Is it just a case of mistaken identity?

After everything that had happened in the past week, the last thing I felt like doing was spending even more time online.

"I should go," I said, checking my watch.

"Hang on," George said. "Don't you want to check your in-box?"

She clicked to open my BetterLife mailbox. As usual since the virtual Incident, there were tons of new e-mails. But another message popped up at that very moment. The sender was someone called UrNewReality, and the subject line read WHAT IS REALITY? "That's different," I said. "Wonder what that's about?"

George clicked on it, and the message text popped up on the screen in what must have been about forty-two-point type.

UNR KNOWS ALL ABOUT U. UNR DOESN'T LIKE U. HOW R U LIKING UR NEW REALITY SO FAR? B/C IT'S ABOUT 2 GET EVEN MORE UNREAL!

NANCY DREW

Available from Aladdin Paperbacks

CAROLYN KEENE

NANCY DREW

GIRL DETECTIVE®

Identity Theft

#34

**Book Two in the
Identity Mystery Trilogy**

Aladdin Paperbacks

New York London Toronto Sydney

This book is a work of fiction. Any references to historical events, real people, or real locales are used fictitiously. Other names, characters, places, and incidents are the product of the author's imagination, and any resemblance to actual events or locales or persons, living or dead, is entirely coincidental.

❧ALADDIN PAPERBACKS
An imprint of Simon & Schuster Children's Publishing Division
1230 Avenue of the Americas, New York, NY 10020
Copyright © 2009 by Simon & Schuster, Inc.
All rights reserved, including the right of
reproduction in whole or in part in any form.
NANCY DREW, NANCY DREW: GIRL DETECTIVE, ALADDIN PAPER-
BACKS, and related logo are registered trademarks of Simon & Schuster, Inc.
Manufactured in the United States of America
First Aladdin Paperbacks edition January 2009
10 9 8 7 6 5 4 3 2 1
Library of Congress Control Number 2008922947
ISBN-13: 978-1-4169-6831-3
ISBN-10: 1-4169-6831-8

Contents

IDENTITY THEFT

HACK TO SQUARE ONE

"**Y**ou can stop apologizing, Nancy. I forgive you, I promise." Ibrahim al-Fulani smiled at me from his seat across the coffee shop table. "I knew you wouldn't have done such a thing. Not someone as nice and kind as you."

I smiled back weakly, clutching my cappuccino with both hands. It was late Saturday morning and Barbara's Beans was crowded, but we'd managed to snag a private table over near the brick wall in the back. That was good. I definitely didn't want half of River Heights to overhear our conversation.

"Thanks, Ibrahim," I said. "Not everyone would be so understanding about this."

That was the understatement of the year. . . . But maybe I'd better back up and explain. For the past week or so I'd been investigating a case involving some cyberbullying that had spilled over into real life. See, that's what I do—investigate. I'm pretty well-known around my hometown of River Heights for being ready, willing, and able to solve any puzzle or mystery, great or small.

And I thought I'd solved this one, too. I'd been called in by a popular middle schooler named Shannon Fitzgerald. She was getting teased and harassed at school after flirting with a certain boy on an online game called BetterLife. In order to get to the bottom of things, I'd signed on to BetterLife myself, creating an avatar named VirtualNancy that looked just like me, from her strawberry-blond hair to her comfortable shoes. My sleuthing had led me all over town. Well, *towns*, actually—both the real and virtual versions of River Heights. In the end, I'd been able to pin the origin of the bullying on Shannon's so-called best friend, Rebecca, who was getting back at her for a previous tiff.

The end, right? Well, not exactly. After delivering both girls, plus a couple of others who'd gotten involved, to the proper authorities—aka their parents—I'd logged on to BetterLife to close out my avatar, only to find my e-mail in-box crammed with angry messages. The game has a feature in which players can post short video clips of their online activities and interactions, and it seemed a lot of people had viewed a video of VirtualNancy harassing Ibrahim's avatar, hatefully telling him to go back to Iran and even spray painting the words GO HOME on his virtual house.

There was just one problem. I hadn't done that. I would *never* have done something like that. For one thing, Ibrahim is a super-nice guy. He's the sixteen-year-old son of a visiting Iranian professor at River Heights University. Due to a mix-up, the al-Fulanis' university housing was delayed for a few weeks, so in the meantime the whole family was staying with the family of my boyfriend, Ned Nickerson. I'd been spending quite a bit of time with Ibrahim and his younger sister, Arij, and they were both great people—smart, friendly, and eager to fit in at the local middle and high schools. Besides that, I'm just not the harassing type (although some of the crooks and lowlifes I've busted in the past might beg to differ, I suppose).

So who *had* done it? I didn't know, but I definitely intended to find out.

Naturally, I'd called Ibrahim immediately to

explain and apologize. He'd agreed to meet me at the coffee shop right away.

"I still don't know how this happened," I mused, staring across the open, airy room at the bank of computer terminals along the front wall. "George says someone must have hacked into my account so he or she could control my avatar and make it do that stuff."

I was referring to George Fayne, one of my best friends, who also happens to be a whiz with computers and anything electronic. She was supposed to meet me at the coffee shop soon, along with her cousin and my other best friend, Bess Marvin.

Checking my watch, I saw that they were due at any moment. We'd arranged to meet at noon, figuring that would give me enough time to apologize to Ibrahim in private.

"Anyway, I hope George can help me figure out exactly how someone did this," I said. "Then it'll be up to me to figure out exactly why."

Ibrahim shrugged and took a sip of his mochaccino. "I have heard that some hackers do it just for the fun and challenge of it—for kicks, as you might say."

"I suppose that's true." As usual, I couldn't help being impressed with Ibrahim's command of

English slang. Then again, he and his family had lived in the United States for a while; Professor al-Fulani had taught at several other universities before being invited to come to River Heights. "But in this case, I'm not so sure that's what's going on. It just seems too coincidental for it to happen just as I'd solved the other mystery."

"Yes, that makes sense." Ibrahim gazed at me with admiration in his dark eyes. "I still find it very cool that you are an amateur detective, Nancy. I'm sure not many people your age can say the same! So do you have any suspects in mind yet?"

"Well . . ." I leaned on one elbow and stirred my drink, staring thoughtfully into the tiny whirlpool I created. "I suppose the obvious place to look would be the middle schoolers I busted for the Shannon business. They're the ones with an obvious motive—revenge."

Rebecca wasn't the only one who'd been in trouble when I turned her in to her parents. Shannon herself hadn't come out smelling like roses, either, since it turned out the whole thing had been prompted by some major bullying on her part. There were also a couple of other middle school girls who'd joined in on Rebecca's plot and probably weren't too happy with me right now.

"Still, this seems pretty extreme for those girls," I mused aloud, thinking over the potential list of suspects. "I mean, we know Shannon is a bully and Rebecca is kind of sneaky, but even so . . ."

I glanced toward the computers again just in time to spot Bess and George hurrying into the coffee shop. As usual, Bess looked pretty and pulled together. She was dressed in a cute floral dress that flattered her curvy figure, and not a hair on her blond head was out of place. George, on the other hand, looked like she'd just pulled an all-nighter. Her short dark hair was standing on end, both her sneakers were untied, and her rumpled T-shirt was only half tucked into the waistband of her jeans. Then again, that was nothing unusual. George cares even less about fashion and makeup than I do, and is a lot less receptive to Bess's constant tips on keeping ourselves presentable.

"Um, hi," Bess greeted us cautiously as the two of them approached our table. "Is everything . . . ?"

"Everything's fine," I said. "Ibrahim is being super-understanding."

"But of course." Ibrahim smiled. "I knew instantly that Nancy would never act in that way toward me or anyone else. And I have every confidence that she will solve this case quickly."

There were only three chairs at our table, so George grabbed an extra one from nearby, turned it around, and straddled it, leaning on the back and staring at me. "Listen," she said. "I've been messing around a little trying to figure out how someone could've snagged your avatar like that. And let me tell you, it's no easy matter to hack into the BetterLife system. Whoever did it must be a real pro."

"Yeah." Bess chuckled. "Or at least more of a pro than George. She's been trying for the past hour and can't get past the first firewall."

George scowled at her. "Give me time," she snapped. "I'll get in. It's just not as easy as most sites, okay?"

I held back a smile. Judging by her reaction, George's failure to break into the game's system had wounded her hacker pride.

"Anyway, I'll keep trying," she went on. "But in the meantime, that Virtual Nancy avatar is pretty much useless—everyone on BetterLife knows her, and she can't go anywhere without getting harassed. I think we should create a new, more anonymous avatar and use it to poke around some."

"Uh-uh." I pushed away my half-empty coffee cup. "I've had just about enough of this virtual sleuthing. I'm going to start this investigation off in the real world by talking to Shannon and Rebecca."

"But I thought you didn't believe they were capable of such a thing," Ibrahim said.

I shrugged. "True. But they both hid what they were up to pretty well last time. So it's worth a shot, if only to cross them off the suspect list."

Bess pursed her lips. "Well, before you do that, maybe you should just check in quickly on the game," she suggested. "There's been, um, a new development since you were on there earlier this morning."

"What do you mean?" I asked.

"Just come on and we'll show you. Look, there's a computer free now." George hopped up and hurried over to commandeer the one empty terminal in the row by the door.

After everything that had happened in the past week, the last thing I felt like doing was spending even more time online. But I couldn't help being curious. I followed my friends over to the computer, with Ibrahim right behind me.

Soon George had us logged on to BetterLife. As usual, up popped an online replica of the real town of River Heights. The sunny, slightly breezy day was also a replica of the real-life day outside the coffee shop windows. Probably the biggest difference between the online and real worlds was that the virtual River Street was a lot busier, with tons of avatars wandering around, interacting and having conversations, which popped up as little text boxes all over the screen.

"Okay, so what are we supposed to be looking at?" I asked, leaning over George's shoulder for a better view.

In response, George's fingers wielded keyboard and mouse as she guided us down the street and around a couple of corners. I recognized Virtual-Nancy's neighborhood, where she had a cute little condo with a river view. There were a bunch of people milling around in front of the door, and for a second I wasn't sure what they were doing there.

Then George zoomed in, and I gasped as I spotted my avatar's name on a placard that one of the virtual people was holding. "Hey," I said. "Are those people *picketing* me?"

"Yup," George said grimly. "They started showing up right after you left to go meet Ibrahim."

I had to pause for a split second to work out whether she was talking about the real or virtual me. That also gave me time to read some of the virtual picket signs. The messages included stuff like VNANCY = JRK, I H8 BIGOTS! and GAL.

"GAL?" I said when I saw the last one. "What's that?"

"It stands for 'get a life,'" George replied.

I grimaced. Nice. "Wow," I said. "People are really taking this seriously."

"Oh, Nancy!" Ibrahim cried. "I'm so sorry—I cannot help feeling responsible for all this."

"Don't be silly, Ibrahim. It's not your fault." I bit my lip as I watched a petite girl with a mohawk and a nose ring march around on the screen carrying a VN IZA IDIOT! sign.

The person at the next computer terminal had just left, and Bess sat down in the vacant seat. "But it's not all bad, Nancy," she said in her glass-half-full way, pointing to one side of the screen. "Some people are supporting you, see?"

Now that she pointed it out, I did. About eighty percent of the picketers appeared to be anti-VirtualNancy. But the rest were actually picketing in my favor, waving signs with slogans like VN IS NO BIGOT! and INNOCENT TIL PROVEN GUILTY!

Somehow, that seemed even weirder than the ones picketing against me. "Who *are* these people?" I murmured, leaning even closer. "I mean, it's a gorgeous day outside, and they could be out there walking in the park by the river or having a picnic or—"

I cut myself off with a gasp as I got a look at the name of one of the pro-VirtualNancy people. Bess must have seen it at the same moment.

"Hey," she said. "Check it out. It's Guitar Lover Fifteen!"

"What's he doing there?" I exclaimed. "Rebecca's mother said she was going to ban her from the computer for at least a month."

I stared at the all-too-familiar avatar of a teenage boy with a blue streak in his dark hair. Guitarlvr15 was the avatar Rebecca had used to torture Shannon online. He was the spitting image of the guy Shannon liked in real life, a sixteen-year-old named Jake.

"Well, someone poached *your* avatar," George pointed out. "Maybe someone grabbed Rebecca's, too."

"Or perhaps Rebecca has sneaked back online somehow," Ibrahim put in.

"But if she had, why would she be picketing *for* Nancy?" Bess wondered. "Wouldn't she be a lot more likely to be giving her a hard time for busting her?"

I shrugged. "Maybe. Unless she created this

whole protest somehow and is just checking it out while staying under the radar."

"Using that avatar isn't exactly staying under the radar," George pointed out. "Why wouldn't she just make another one?"

"Good point." I quickly scanned some of the other pro-VirtualNancy picketers. A couple of them seemed vaguely familiar—I suspected one might be a college student I knew from one of my charity committees, while another looked a lot like my friend Charlie Adams, who worked at a local garage.

But most were complete strangers, at least as far as I could tell. Then again, who knew? It wasn't as if people were restricted to making their online avatars look or act like their real-life selves. In BetterLife, they could be anyone or anything they wanted to be. The attractive twentyish woman in the miniskirt and go-go boots waving her VN ROX! sign could actually be a ten-year-old boy. That petite punk rocker might be, say, Chief McGinnis of the River Heights Police. The pro-VirtualNancy avatar that looked like a Scandinavian male model and called himself MrNiceGuy might actually belong to a pudgy middle-aged accountant.

Then I spotted another pro-me avatar. This one

was a college-aged guy, tall and broad-shouldered and good-looking. He was carrying an I ♥ VN sign and his name was NedNick02.

I was a little surprised. True, Ned had mentioned that he had an avatar on BetterLife. But so far he hadn't seemed all that interested in spending much time on the site. Still, it was nice to see my boyfriend there sticking up for me, especially considering the way I'd been canceling our dates lately due to Shannon's case.

That reminded me—Ned and I were supposed to have dinner that very night. If I wanted to question Shannon and Rebecca and still have time to find something date-appropriate to wear, I had to get moving.

"I should go," I said, checking my watch. "I want to see if Shannon knows anything about all this."

"Hang on," George said. "Don't you want to check your in-box?"

I made a face. "Why bother? I already know what most of the messages are going to say."

But I watched as George clicked to open my BetterLife mailbox. As usual since the virtual Incident, there were tons of new e-mails. Most of them featured subject lines like OMG UR A RACIST!!1! or Y R U SUCH A H8R?!?!?!

"Come on, enough," I said. "Just log off so we can . . ."

My voice trailed off as yet another message popped up at that very moment. The sender was someone called UrNewReality, and the subject line read WHAT IS REALITY?

"That's different," I said, relieved to see at least one message that wasn't calling me names in the subject line. "Wonder what that's about?"

George clicked on it, and the message text popped up on the screen in what must have been about forty-two-point type.

UNR KNOWS ALL ABOUT U. UNR DOESN'T LIKE U. HOW R U LIKING UR NEW REALITY SO FAR? B/C IT'S ABOUT 2 GET EVEN MORE UNREAL!

THREATENING WORDS

"**U**h-oh," Ibrahim said with a worried frown. "I do not like the sound of that." I shrugged, reaching over to click away from the message. "Forget it," I said. "I don't like being threatened, and I've had enough of messing around online. It's time to clear my name—in *real* life."

But Ibrahim still looked concerned. "Listen, Nancy," he said sincerely. "I do not think you should brush this off. Unfortunately, I do have some experience with threats of this sort."

For a moment I assumed he was referring to what I—or, rather, my virtual self—had done to him. But before I could start apologizing again, he went on.

"My father, he is known for getting people riled up by speaking frankly about race, religion, Middle Eastern policy, that sort of thing," he said, his usual happy-go-lucky expression replaced by a much more somber one. "He means no harm by this, of course."

"Of course," I agreed. "He's only trying to make people think—challenge their assumptions and that sort of thing."

George nodded. "Like an Iranian version of Martin Luther King or someone." At my surprised glance, she shrugged. "What? I do read a newspaper once in a while, you know."

"You do?" Bess sounded surprised, too.

George grinned. "Sure. The online version still counts, right?"

Ibrahim sighed, hardly seeming to hear our banter. "But you see, not everyone appreciates having their assumptions challenged, Nancy, and that is the problem. In the past, his speeches have been picketed many times. We have had insulting and sometimes frightening letters mailed to our home, and had Homeland Security called on us for no reason." He shrugged and glanced down at the floor, kicking lightly at the leg of the computer stand. "Once, a protester even jumped onstage during a speech and tried to punch my father in the nose."

Wow. My own father, Carson Drew, was a successful and fairly high-profile attorney, and had seen his share of angry opponents and threats. But I couldn't imagine what it would be like to deal with the sort of thing Ibrahim was describing.

"I'm so sorry, Ibrahim." Bess put a hand on his arm. "I hope none of those things have happened since your family came to River Heights."

"Not yet," Ibrahim said. "And I do hope it will be different here—this is a very nice town and everyone has been so kind to us. However, my father has just told us . . ." He glanced around the crowded coffee shop and lowered his voice. "You will not tell anyone what I am about to say?"

"Of course not," I said while George nodded and Bess crossed her heart.

Ibrahim took a deep breath. "My father just told us he is planning to announce on Monday that he will give the keynote speech on Friday evening at the university to kick off International Peace Week."

I'd heard about International Peace Week, of course. In fact, one of my volunteer groups was helping with the local event's publicity and event planning, and I'd spent an entire afternoon a month or two earlier stuffing envelopes to ask for donations. I hadn't heard that Professor al-Fulani would be the keynote speaker, but I wasn't surprised. His message of tolerance and education was right up Peace Week's alley.

"I appreciate your concern, Ibrahim." I smiled sympathetically. "But I really don't think one anonymous e-mail on an online game site rises to the same level as the issues your father has to deal with."

Bess pursed her lips. "You're probably right, Nancy," she said with a hint of doubt in her voice. "But maybe you should mention it to your dad, just in case."

"Or even report it to the cops," George put in. "They take this online harassment stuff pretty seriously these days."

I shrugged. "Maybe so. But one rude e-mail doesn't exactly constitute harassment. Besides, my dad is totally preoccupied with some huge new case he just took on involving a major drug bust over in Silver Creek." Glancing at George, I smiled. "And I can only imagine what Chief McGinnis might say if I came to him with something like this."

Ibrahim looked a bit confused at that, but Bess and George both chuckled. Our local police chief isn't my biggest fan, mostly because I have a habit of solving his cases more quickly than he does.

I stood up. "Anyway, I suspect this is nothing but overflow from the case we just solved. Let's go pay a visit to Shannon and find out for sure."

Leaving Ibrahim at the computer terminal checking in on his own BetterLife avatar, my friends and I hurried outside. My Prius was parked at the curb right in front of the coffee shop.

"Looks like my meter's almost out," I said. "I might as well drive."

Bess and George exchanged an anxious glance. "Um, are you sure you don't want me to drive?" Bess asked, gesturing to her own car parked half-way down the block. "I don't mind."

"Yeah." George fished in her pockets. "I probably have some change on me to feed your meter."

I rolled my eyes. For some reason, my friends don't trust my driving. And if George was actually offering to part with some of her own hard-earned money to prevent me from driving, she had to be even more nervous about it than usual.

But I wasn't in the mood to worry about my friends' peculiarities at the moment.

"Don't be silly," I said, already pointing the keyless entry remote at the car. "Hop in."

Soon we were tooling along toward Shannon's house, which was located in a nice, leafy neighborhood at the edge of town. As I maneuvered through the Saturday-afternoon traffic, George slouched in the front seat and fiddled with my cell phone, which I'd left on the dashboard.

"That message from the Your New Reality guy was pretty weird," she commented. "If you don't want to go to your dad or whatever, maybe you should forward the e-mail to BetterLife's community bulletin board."

Bess leaned forward from the backseat. "That's a great idea," she agreed. "Maybe it would help convince people you weren't the one who did that horrible stuff to Ibrahim."

I rolled my eyes. "Great. A virtual solution to a virtual problem," I quipped. The bulletin board they were talking about was a sort of virtual kiosk where BetterLife members could post news, notices, invitations, or anything else they wanted to share with the entire BetterLife community.

"Think about it, Nancy," Bess urged. "You

don't want to let everyone go on thinking the worst of you, do you?"

"Actually, if this UrNewReality character is someone other than Shannon or Rebecca, it's probably better if he thinks he scared me with that stupid threat, at least until I can figure out his real ID." I shrugged. "Besides, who cares what a bunch of pixels on a screen think of me? It's just a game."

George and Bess traded a dubious look. "Oh, really?" George said. "Tell that to Shannon and her little friends."

"True," Bess agreed. "BetterLife overflowed into the real world before, and lots of people got their real-life feelings hurt over it, remember?"

I did. But I still wasn't going to let that scare me. "Look, I see your point," I told them. "But I'm still living in the real world, and as long as there aren't real-life picketers outside my real-life house, I'm not going to worry too much about what people choose to do behind the anonymity of a computer screen."

"Well, just don't forget that not everybody draws such a sharp distinction between real life and online life anymore," George warned. "A lot of people are really into this so-called game. For instance, you're not the only one getting picketed lately—a bunch of BetterLifers have started protesting the paid subscription thing."

"Really? I hadn't heard about that," I said, accelerating through a yellow light as I thought over what I knew about the upcoming launch of a new, upgraded, paid version of BetterLife. It was supposed to have exciting new features, more video capability, and all kinds of other cool stuff that most people claimed would make the free version all but obsolete. According to George, the creators stood to make billions from it.

"Wait," Bess put in. "Do you mean people are protesting on the site, or in real life?"

"Both, I think." George shrugged. "Definitely on the site—I've seen them doing that. But I heard a few diehards are camped out in front of Robert Sung's and Jack Crilley's houses."

"Really? Why?" Bess sounded as astonished as I felt.

George shrugged again. "I don't know. I guess they don't like change. Or maybe they're afraid it'll cost too much. Some people just seem to feel like Crilley and Sung are selling out or something."

I shook my head, not sure whether to be amused or amazed that people let an online game affect them so much. Either way, I felt a flash of sympathy for the two creators of BetterLife. Getting picketed online was bad enough; it had to totally stink in real life. Before I could comment, my cell phone rang in George's hand.

She glanced at it. "It's Ned," she reported. Hitting a button, she put it on speaker and answered. "Nancy Drew's secretary speaking. How may I direct your call?"

"Very funny. Give it here." I held out my hand.

"Are you sure you can talk and drive at the same time?" George asked.

I grabbed the phone from her, leaving it on speaker. "Ned? Hey, sorry about that."

I expected him to chuckle, as he normally would at George's antics. But when he spoke, he sounded kind of tense.

"Hi, Nancy. I know this is a long shot, but have you seen Ibrahim lately?" he asked.

"Sure," I replied, balancing the phone between my hand and the steering wheel as I turned onto Union Street. "I just left him at Barbara's Beans. Why?"

"You did?" Ned sounded surprised—and maybe a bit disgruntled. Or was that my imagination? "Um, okay. Do you think he's still there? Because it's really important that I find him as soon as possible."

"He's probably still there. Why, what's up?"

This time when he answered, Ned sounded downright grim. "His family wants him home immediately because his father just received a very serious threat."

A BAD CALL

"A threat?" I repeated in surprise. "What are you talking about?"

"What threat?" George hissed, looking concerned.

"Shh," I hushed her, switching the phone to my other hand and ignoring the resulting gasp from Bess as I took both hands off the steering wheel for a second. "What's going on, Ned? Does this have something to do with BetterLife?"

"BetterLife? No, of course not," Ned said. "Well, at least not really."

"Huh?" I said.

Bess poked me in the shoulder. "What's going on?" she whispered.

I flapped a hand to shush her. "Fill me in, please, Ned. Who's making these threats, and why?"

"Someone called Professor al-Fulani's office at the university because they'd just heard he'll be speaking at Peace Week."

I nodded, then blinked as I remembered how Ibrahim had sworn us to secrecy just now. "Wait, I thought that wasn't going to be announced until Monday," I said.

"So did the professor. But someone found out and leaked it a couple of days early. It was posted on the BetterLife bulletin board less than an hour ago." Ned sighed. "And apparently some people aren't happy about the news. It's causing quite an uproar on campus; protesters are already out in force in front of the professor's office, both pro and con."

I let out a low whistle and asked, "Has the family called the police?"

"Of course," Ned replied. "They seem to think it was probably just a crank call, but they're looking into it just in case. Meanwhile the professor and his wife are understandably anxious to make sure their kids are both home and safe—Arij is already here, but they're worried about Ibrahim, especially since he forgot his cell phone today and they can't reach him. Anyway, I guess the whole family has dealt with some problems like this before."

"I know," I said, flashing back again to the conversation in the coffee shop. "Ibrahim was just telling us about that."

"Hmm." Ned cleared his throat. "Anyway, I'd better hang up and go pick him up at the coffee shop."

"Don't bother. I can go back and get him," I offered, already checking my rearview to see if it was safe to make a U-turn.

"No, that's okay," Ned said quickly. "Now that I know where he is, I'll just drive over there myself and bring him back here."

"But I'm only, like, three minutes from the coffee shop," I protested. "It'll be much quicker if I—"

"Thanks, but I'm on it. Oh, and listen—is it okay if I take a rain check on dinner tonight? I have a feeling this situation is going to turn into an all-day thing."

"Sure," I said. "Totally understood. We'll reschedule once things settle down."

"Cool. Later, Nancy."

He hung up before I could say anything else. I hit the End button and tossed my phone back to George, surprised that Ned had turned down my offer to fetch Ibrahim. The Nickersons' house was at least a ten-minute drive from the coffee shop at this time of day; by the time Ned got there, I could've already had Ibrahim halfway home.

"Wow," George said. "Guess Ibrahim wasn't kidding about people having it in for his dad."

Bess nodded. "And more protests, too," she said. "Weird."

"I know. It's like the craziness of BetterLife is spilling out into the real world, just like you guys were saying."

"So you're rescheduling yet again?" Bess asked.

I should have known she'd catch that. Bess is a hopeless romantic.

"Uh-huh." I shrugged and smiled weakly. "Hey, but at least this time it's not my fault, right?" I still felt guilty about canceling on Ned so often lately. "Talk about bad timing, though—it's starting to feel like we haven't spent any quality alone time together in eons."

"Maybe you should send VirtualNancy out to snuggle with Ned's avatar, since he's picketing right outside your—I mean her—house," George joked.

"Right." Bess rolled her eyes. "A virtual date. How very romantic."

George grinned. "Hey, it's better than nothing, right?"

I wasn't too sure about that. But I didn't have time to ponder it, since we were already turning onto Shannon's block. As I pulled the car to the curb in front of her house, I saw two women standing on the front porch. One of them was Shannon's mother, a slender, pretty blond who looked just as Shannon herself probably would in twenty or thirty years. The second woman was heavyset, with dark hair and a heavily lined face. She appeared to be a few years older than Mrs. Fitzgerald, and was wearing a shapeless, old-fashioned dress that even my style-challenged self didn't need Bess to tell me was hopelessly frumpy.

My friends and I headed up the front walk. The women spotted us, and I thought I saw Mrs. Fitzgerald frown slightly and murmur something to her companion.

"Er, hello again, Nancy," she said when we got closer. "I didn't expect to see you again today."

I was surprised by her slightly hostile tone. It had been only a matter of hours since I'd seen her last, and at the time she'd been tired and upset but also grateful to me for getting to the bottom of the situation with her daughter.

Even though Shannon was grounded from BetterLife, could Mrs. Fitzgerald have already heard about the problem? "Um," I said awkwardly, "you didn't happen to hear about my avatar's latest escapades on BetterLife, did you? Because you see, it actually wasn't me at all. That's why I'm here, in fact. . . ." I went on to explain the whole story with Ibrahim and my hijacked avatar.

Even before I finished, I could see Mrs. Fitzgerald's expression relax, though the other woman continued to stare at me with open curiosity. "Oh, I see," Mrs. Fitzgerald said when I'd finished. "What a relief. I should have known you wouldn't do that, Nancy. But honestly, these days it's getting hard to know just what anyone will do, especially if they think they can hide behind their keyboard. . . ."

I smiled sympathetically, guessing that she was thinking about her own daughter's actions and those of her friends. "I hear you," I said. "It's a whole new world out there, isn't it?"

"Yes, indeed. Oh! But where are my manners?" the woman said. "Nancy Drew, this is my sister-in-law, Agnes Fitzgerald. She stopped by to visit Shannon as soon as she heard what happened." She smiled sheepishly. "I know Shannon's supposed to be grounded from all visitors, but I figured family doesn't count. Besides, Agnes and Shannon have always been close, and we hope she'll be a good influence on her at this time."

"Nice to meet you, Ms. Fitzgerald," I said politely, holding out my hand. Aunt Agnes just stared at it for a moment as if not certain what she was supposed to do with it.

"Oh," she said after a moment, finally taking my hand and giving it a quick, listless shake. "Uh, hello."

I introduced Bess and George as well, then turned back to Mrs. Fitzgerald. "Anyway, I know you just said no visitors. But I was actually hoping I could talk to Shannon. It would only take a few minutes."

Mrs. Fitzgerald smiled. "Of course, Nancy. We can certainly make an exception for you after all you've done."

"Excuse me," Aunt Agnes said abruptly. "I have to go. Don't want to be late for work."

"All right." Mrs. Fitzgerald patted the older woman on the arm. "Thanks for stopping by. I'm sure Shannon appreciated the friendly face."

That wasn't quite how I would have described dour Agnes Fitzgerald myself. Still, I supposed "friendly" was in the eye of the beholder.

"Nice to meet you, Ms. Fitzgerald," Bess said politely.

Aunt Agnes nodded, then hurried down the steps, making her way toward a shabby-looking minivan parked at the curb right in front of my Prius. Shannon's mother waved until the other woman climbed in and drove off in a cloud of exhaust. Then she turned to lead us into the house.

"Agnes works in the cafeteria over at the university," she said conversationally as she opened the door. "I wouldn't enjoy working so many weekends myself, but it seems to suit her." She glanced up the stairs leading to the second floor. "Go on upstairs to Shannon's room—you know where it is."

"Thanks," I said, taking the steps two at a time with my friends at my heels.

Shannon seemed less than thrilled to see me again. "Oh," she said when she opened her bedroom door and peered out. "It's you."

"It's me," I replied lightly. "You remember Bess, right? And this is our friend George. May we come in?"

Shannon stared at George. "Your name is George?" she demanded. "What's that about?"

"What's it to you?" George countered.

I cleared my throat. "Er, listen, Shannon," I

said. "We won't stay long. But I need to talk to you about what's been going on this morning on BetterLife."

Shannon blinked. "What do you mean?"

"I mean the way someone hacked my character and made her do stuff I'd never do—like attack a friend and tell him to go back to Iran." I watched Shannon carefully for any hint of recognition or guilt.

Instead, she looked genuinely surprised. "Really?" she said. "Whoa, that's harsh."

"I know. And since I know you're probably not exactly pleased with me right now . . ."

"You mean you think *I* did it?" Shannon rolled her eyes. "Um, duh! Did you already forget that you got me banned from the computer for, like, *ever*?" She scowled and flopped down on the edge of her bed. "Even my aunt thinks it's totally unfair, and she's super-old and stuff."

No wonder poor Aunt Agnes looked so grumpy just now, I thought, holding back a smile. *She probably had to spend the whole morning listening to Shannon singing a full chorus of oh-poor-me.*

"So you don't know anything about this?" George demanded, narrowing her eyes at Shannon. "What about your little friends? Think they might've done it?"

"How should I know?" Shannon shot back, still sounding disgruntled. "I'm not allowed to see them. Or call them. Or even text them. I haven't talked to anyone outside my stupid family for, like, a whole day now."

Bess shrugged. "Well, we were just wondering," she said. "See, our old friend Guitarlvr15 showed up on BetterLife this morning."

"Really?" Shannon looked mildly interested. "Well, I can pretty much guarantee it's not Rebecca this time. Her mom's way strict—even worse than mine. She's probably chained in the basement or something to keep her away from the computer."

I'd met Rebecca's parents, and they didn't seem like the chaining-in-the-basement type. However, they did seem strict enough that it was unlikely that Rebecca could have wriggled out of her punishment, especially so soon.

"All right," I said, heading for the door. "Thanks for talking to us, Shannon."

"Whatever." Shannon was already reaching for the magazine lying on her bed.

We went downstairs and said good-bye to Mrs. Fitzgerald. "I hope she wasn't too cranky?" she asked with a wry smile.

I chuckled. "Only a little," I said. "I'm sure it's

not easy being cut off from her friends like that at her age."

"So she keeps telling me," Mrs. Fitzgerald agreed with a grimace. "But it's the only way they'll learn. Fortunately all the involved parents are in full agreement on that. And no matter what Shannon or the others think, being off-line for a while won't kill them!"

Soon my friends and I were outside heading toward my car. "So?" Bess said. "Do you believe her, Nancy?"

"You mean Shannon? Yeah, I think I do." I shrugged. "Not that she's proven herself terribly trustworthy or anything, but I doubt there's any way she could have sneaked online with her family riding her like that. Not so soon."

"True," George agreed, kicking at a loose stone on the path. "Sounds like the other parents are the same way."

"But what about the Guitarlvr15 thing?" Bess asked. "Pretty weird that he'd show up again so soon."

"Yeah, I'll definitely be checking that out," I agreed. "In the meantime, though, it might be time to start thinking about new suspects." I sighed as I realized what that meant. "I guess I should start by investigating some of the people protesting against me on BetterLife."

"It's strange, all these protests, isn't it?" Bess mused. "The ones outside your virtual place, the ones against the creators of the game, and now the ones Ned was telling you about at the university . . ."

"You don't think there's any connection, do you?" George wrinkled her nose. "What do some jerks who don't like Professor al-Fulani have to do with Nancy?"

Bess shrugged. "Well, it was his son that she supposedly harassed, right? Coincidence, or not?"

We'd reached the car by now, and George reached for the passenger-side handle. "Hang on," I said, stepping closer. "I need to unlock— oops, never mind," I corrected myself. "Looks like I forgot to lock it."

"You, forget something like that?" Bess laughed. "Say it isn't so, Nancy!"

I smiled weakly. While anyone who knows me would agree that my mind is a steel trap when it comes to solving mysteries, even I had to admit that other, less important details sometimes fell by the wayside when I was on a case. I'd been known to leave the house with mismatched sneakers—more than once, actually. Forgetting to lock my car was nothing.

"Come on," I said, climbing into the driver's seat and pulling on my seat belt. "Maybe we should swing by the university and check out those protests for ourselves—just in case."

When everyone was inside, I punched the button on the dashboard to start the car. I jumped as the car emitted a loud, piercing *BEEP! BEEP! BEEP!*

"Who forgot their seat belt?" I asked, automatically glancing over at George. But she was strapped in properly, and when I looked in the backseat, Bess was, too.

"What's wrong with it?" Bess exclaimed, raising her voice to be heard over the continuous shrill beeping.

I shrugged, hitting the power button again to turn off the car, then once more to turn it back on. But the same thing happened. As soon as the car powered on, that insistent beeping started up again.

"Guess I'd better call the shop," I said, hitting the button again to make the noise stop. "Toss me my phone, George. The garage number's on auto-dial."

"Okay. Where'd you put it?"

"What do you mean? I thought you had it," I replied.

"I set it back on the dashboard before we got out to go into Shannon's house," George said. "Did you grab it after that?"

"No." I patted my pockets to make sure. "If you don't have it, and I don't have it, and Bess doesn't have it"—I shot a glance back at Bess, who shook her head—"then what happened to my phone?"

DANGER IN NUMBERS

"**D**o you think someone saw the phone sitting there and stole it?" Bess exclaimed. "I mean, the doors *were* unlocked. . . ."

"Why would anyone bother?" George said. "Her phone's not exactly top-of-the-line."

"Gee, thanks." I was already leaning down, peering at the floor to see if it might have fallen. "Check around before we panic, okay?"

George bent down. "Hang on—here it is," she exclaimed, fishing down by her feet. "It was, like, wedged in under the seat. I didn't even see it when I got in."

"That's weird." Bess leaned forward between the seats. "Do you think you knocked it down when you got out of the car before?"

George shrugged. "It's possible, I guess," she said doubtfully. "I don't know. I didn't notice anything."

I bit my lip, glancing from the phone in George's hand to the car's start button. "I hate to sound paranoid," I began slowly, "but what if someone knocked it down while they were in here messing around with my car?"

"You mean someone might've tampered with the car's computer system?" George's eyes widened. "Yeah, that would certainly explain the beeping, wouldn't it?"

"And what if it's not just beeping?" Suddenly Bess sounded nervous. "This whole car is, like, controlled by a computer, right? Who knows what could happen if someone fiddled with it?"

Despite her girly looks and interests, Bess is actually a pretty handy mechanic, but she's never quite trusted my high-tech hybrid. Still, she did have a point this time.

"Given what's been happening lately, I guess we shouldn't take any chances," I said with a sigh. "I'll call the garage and see if they can come tow us in and give it a look."

I called the garage, and then we climbed out and sat on the curb to wait for the tow truck.

"Okay, if this turns out to be connected to the case, I guess Shannon's off the hook," I said, stretching out my legs and glancing up and down the street. The Fitzgeralds' neighborhood was quiet at the moment, with neither traffic nor pedestrians in sight, let alone any likely suspects. "Do you think someone could have followed us here from the coffee shop?"

"But why?" Bess asked dubiously. "The Better-Life thing is the only case you've been working on lately, right? Do you really think this could be connected to that?"

"Maybe. That UrNewReality message *did* sound like a threat." I shrugged. "Then again, maybe it has something to do with Ibrahim, or his father. Some people obviously have it in for the professor. Maybe someone saw us with Ibrahim and decided it would be fun to make trouble for his friends, too."

"Seems like a stretch," George said bluntly. Then her eyes widened. "But hey, what about that big case your dad's working on? Didn't you say it was like a drug bust or something? What if you're being targeted because of that?"

"I suppose it's possible," I agreed. "But Dad definitely would have mentioned it if he thought I might be in any danger."

"*If* he realized it," George said darkly. "Some of those drug types are scary, Nance. You'd better watch your back if you think they could be involved."

"Or maybe your wacky Jetsons car just shorted out one of its circuits, and this is all a big coincidence," Bess put in. "I mean, I'm still worried about that UrNewReality thing, too. But let's not fly off in a panic, okay?"

"Yeah." My mind was still turning over what had just happened, trying to make sense of it. Coincidence? Maybe. But I had a hunch there was more to it than that.

Moments later Charlie Adams pulled up in the tow truck from Carr's Garage. Charlie is a few years old than me and has been working for the garage since the day he turned sixteen. He's bailed me out of car trouble on numerous occasions—so numerous, in fact, that he doesn't even charge me for the tow half the time. My friends seem to think that's because he has a crush on me, but I choose to ignore that possibility and just consider Charlie a good friend.

"Hi, Nancy," he said, smiling at me and then lifting a hand to wave at Bess and George as he hopped down from the cab of the truck. "Got here as fast as I could. Want me to drop you guys off at home on my way back to the garage? They can call you once the guys take a look at your car."

"Thanks, Charlie," I said. "Actually, if you wouldn't mind, can you drop us in front of Barbara's Beans instead? Bess's car is parked there."

"Sure thing. Just let me get hooked up, and we're on our way."

"Okay, where to now?" Bess asked as she put her car in gear.

Charlie had just dropped us off. Barbara's Beans was busier than ever, but a quick look inside had showed us that Ibrahim was long gone.

"I still wouldn't mind heading to the university," I said, leaning back in the front passenger seat.

"You mean to check out the protests?" George asked from the back. "Good idea."

"That, too," I said as Bess pulled out into traffic. "But I also want to see if we can track down Shannon's aunt at the dining hall."

"Aunt Agnes?" George wrinkled her nose. "Why? You want to ask her to be your new BFF or something? She wasn't exactly Ms. Personality."

"She was parked right in front of my car,

remember?" I said. "I want to see if she noticed anyone hanging around when she left. You know, a mysterious-looking gardener or delivery man, maybe a stranger lurking in the neighbor's landscaping . . ."

Bess nodded. "Good call," she said. "We weren't inside for all that long—maybe twenty minutes, tops. If someone did mess with your car, they must've worked fast. Maybe she did see something."

It only took a few minutes to reach the tidy, attractive campus of River Heights University. Bess parked her car in a public lot, then we headed through the tall iron gates with their anvil insignia onto the college green.

"Whoa," George said, staring across the neatly tended lawn toward a cluster of ivy-draped brick buildings on the far side. "Ned wasn't kidding about the protests."

I followed her gaze. There had to be at least sixty or seventy people marching around in front of one particular building. "Let's get closer," I said, already hurrying forward.

When we joined the curious crowd gathering around the picketers, I could see that at least seventy-five percent of the protesters were actually students and others holding hastily scribbled signs in support of Professor al-Fulani. That made sense—even though he'd only been there a week, I'd heard the visiting professor was already popular with students. Most of the people in this group were laughing, singing, and generally treating the whole thing as a lark.

"That's college kids for ya," George quipped. "What's more fun than a good old-fashioned Saturday-afternoon protest? Well, except maybe playing Hacky Sack . . ."

Next my gaze turned to the opposing side. Those protesting against the professor, while fewer in number, seemed to be taking things much more seriously. Their signs were larger and more brightly painted, with angry messages including stuff like AMERICA: LOVE IT OR LEAVE IT! and MIND YOUR OWN BUSINESS!

"Looks like some people took offense at the professor's comments about the United States," George commented.

"Too bad they missed the point," Bess said. "Maybe if they'd listened a little closer, they'd realize he thinks this country is great. In fact, he cares enough about it to want to help make it even better."

I nodded, recognizing several local cranks and troublemakers. Most of them weren't the type to appreciate such nuances. There was Millard Morton, who'd sued city hall at least a dozen times over various matters, from potholes in the street in front of his house to slow pizza delivery—my father had defended the city pro bono on most of those cases. Then we had LuAnn Carter, who loved to call up all the local radio stations to rant about having to press One for English at the local cash machines. I spotted a few more familiar faces, too, though there were also some students and strangers among the picketers. Meanwhile the crowd of curious onlookers seemed to be growing by the minute.

As my friends and I joined that crowd, I recognized another familiar face—Aisha Beck, a talented young reporter for the *River Heights Bugle*. Ned's father was the publisher of the paper, and Ned himself worked there part-time in between his college classes. I'd met Aisha on several occasions and found her smart, tough, and fair.

"Hi, Aisha," I said, hurrying over.

"Oh! Hey, Nancy. Good to see you." The reporter smiled and greeted my friends as well.

I glanced over as the picketers started a chant. "You here covering all the excitement?" I asked Aisha.

"Actually, we found out that Professor al-Fulani

is calling a press conference to address all this." She waved a hand at the action. "Mr. N. sent me right over to get the scoop. Of course, I'm not sure what good it's going to do reporting it in the paper—looks like the entire city's already here!"

My friends and I chuckled. Bess made some response, but I barely heard it. I'd just spotted Shannon's aunt standing at the edge of the crowd nearby, along with a short, skinny woman around her age wearing a hairnet. I guessed the second woman was a coworker at the dining hall, which was just a few doors down from the steps of the building where they were standing to get a better view of the proceedings.

"Excuse me, you guys," I said hastily. "I'll be back in a sec."

Not bothering to wait for a response, I hurried off, winding my way through the still-growing crowd. This seemed like as good a time as any to talk to Aunt Agnes. My years of amateur sleuthing had taught me that witnesses are like seafood meals—best when they're fresh. I wanted to catch Aunt Agnes when she was still likely to remember anything suspicious she might have seen in front of Shannon's house, before the novelty and gossip of the protest and press conference drove it from her mind.

I'd almost reached her when a buzz went up from the crowd. Glancing over my shoulder, I saw that Professor al-Fulani had just emerged onto the front steps of the main university building along with a couple of uniformed security guards and several other people. To my surprise, his wife and children weren't among them. I realized why when I turned back toward Aunt Agnes and spotted the professor's family on the steps of the same building where she and her friend were standing. In fact, only a couple of people separated the al-Fulanis from the two women. If I hadn't been so intent on Aunt Agnes, I might have spotted the al-Fulanis earlier. It looked as if they'd just stepped out of the building behind them, which held several university offices along with some classrooms.

The professor's wife was standing straight and tall, only the slightly pinched expression on the face beneath her hijab giving away the fact that there was anything wrong. Ibrahim and Arij were standing on either side of their mother, both of them looking anxious. I waved, but none of them noticed—their gazes were trained on Professor al-Fulani as he fiddled with the microphone someone had just handed him.

"Welcome," the professor said in his cultured

English, the microphone carrying his voice easily across the green. "Although it is unfortunate to meet under these circumstances, I am still very glad for the chance to speak with all of you today. . . ."

I turned and continued on as he spoke, finally reaching Aunt Agnes, who was watching the professor. "Hello there," I said, touching her on the arm. "Remember me? Nancy Drew? We met a little while ago at your niece's house."

She turned to me and blinked. "Oh," she said. "Uh, okay."

Deciding to take that as a "Yes, lovely to see you again," I continued. "Something kind of weird happened while I was there, and I noticed you were parked in front of me, so—"

"Look out!" Agnes shouted hoarsely, suddenly leaping past me.

I spun around just in time to see her grab Arij al-Fulani by the shoulders and give her a hard shove off the building's steps!

5

TOO MUCH REALITY

"Arij!" the professor's wife cried as both she and Ibrahim leaped toward Arij, who had tumbled to the grass with a startled shriek. I rushed over as well, making the three-foot jump down off the side of the steps and landing at the twelve-year-old girl's side just as she climbed to her feet.

"Are you okay?" I asked, taking her arm to steady her.

"I—I think so, Nancy," she said, her voice shaky. "Thank you. What just happened?"

The university security officers who'd been standing near the family had already grabbed Agnes Fitzgerald. "I'm sorry!" the woman was exclaiming loudly. "I was just trying to help her; I didn't know what else to do. I saw one of those red laser dots moving around on that girl's face, like someone was sighting a rifle at her!"

"What?" The senior security officer looked grim. He gestured to the other guards. "Get them all inside." Then he grabbed a walkie-talkie from his belt and started speaking rapidly to whomever was on the other end.

Before I quite knew what was happening, I was being swept into the building along with Aunt Agnes, the al-Fulanis, and everyone else in the vicinity. Things were chaotic for the next few minutes as the guards started searching and questioning Agnes and everyone else who'd been nearby. I had to wait a few minutes for my turn, and found myself wishing I hadn't forgotten to grab my cell phone out of the car before leaving it at the garage. My friends were probably wondering where I was.

"Did you see anything, miss?" an earnest-looking guard with a freckled face and a prominent Adam's apple finally asked me. He looked so young he could have passed as a freshman at the university.

"Not really," I said. "Did you guys question Aunt Agnes already? Er, I mean Agnes Fitzgerald?"

The young guard looked confused. "Um, what?" he said. Then he frowned. "Wait, I'll ask the questions, if you don't mind. Now, did you notice this red laser thingie while you were outside?"

I shook my head. "No, but I wasn't looking at Arij when it happened. Actually, I was talking with Agnes. But listen, did she say whether she could tell what direction it might be coming from?"

"Hey," the guard exclaimed uncertainly. "Didn't I just speak to you about—"

"It's all right, Maxwell." A tall, blond woman cut him off as she strode briskly up to us. "I'll take over from here if you don't mind."

I smiled with relief. "Hi, Detective Johansen," I greeted the longtime police officer, one of my favorites on the River Heights force, as the young guard wandered off. "So what's going on here? Was the professor's family really in any danger?"

"Wish I knew, Nancy." She shrugged. "The press conference is over, obviously, and we're searching all the buildings for a possible sniper. So far, nothing." She winked. "But you didn't hear it from me, okay?"

"My lips are sealed." I smiled at her. "Thanks. So is my interview over?"

"Sure. You're free to go, Nancy. My best to your father, okay?"

"Absolutely." I waved to her then turned away, wondering if there was any chance of me getting to talk to Aunt Agnes at this point.

Just then the crowd parted slightly and I spotted Ned standing just ahead. I hurried over to him.

"Nancy!" he greeted me, his forehead creased with worry. "This is nuts, huh?"

"Yeah, no wonder you were so anxious to find Ibrahim earlier," I exclaimed.

"Uh, yeah." He frowned slightly.

I bit my lip, belatedly realizing how that might have sounded. For some reason, Ned seemed to think I was spending too much time with Ibrahim. That was crazy, of course—I was just being friendly. But it was weird to think that Ned might actually be jealous. He normally wasn't the type. At least I hadn't thought he was.

"Hey, listen," I blurted out, trying to head off any possible misunderstanding. "I was thinking—should we reschedule that date for next Friday night?"

He blinked, looking surprised. "What? Oh, uh, sure, I guess. Friday sounds good."

"Ned!" Just then Aisha Beck rushed up to us.

"Listen, I think I just convinced the cops to let me interview the woman who shoved the al-Fulani girl. Can you see if you can talk to Chief McGinnis, get him to make a statement?"

"I'm on it," Ned replied immediately. He shot me one last glance. "Friday," he said.

"Friday," I repeated, though I wasn't sure he heard me as he disappeared into the crowd.

"So you were standing right there when it happened?" Bess asked as she spun the wheel to make the turn onto River Street.

"What can I say? I have a knack for being in the right place at the right time," I quipped. I'd just finished telling my friends about what had happened.

"Red laser dot, huh?" George mused from the backseat. "That doesn't necessarily mean it was a rifle sighting on her. It could've been one of those laser pointer gizmos. Lots of professors at the university use them, and anyone else could get one easily enough."

I nodded. "I thought of that. Even so, it still seems suspicious that it would be trained on Arij at that particular moment. Maybe someone's trying to scare her—or, rather, her dad."

"Could be," Bess agreed. "Poor thing! Imagine

having to deal with all this at age twelve."

"I know." I sighed. "I can't help feeling guilty about it, too."

"You? Why?" George asked.

I shrugged, glancing out the car window as we passed Barbara's Beans. "I know it's silly. But I can't help wondering if I—or, rather, my latest case—might have contributed even slightly to what happened today."

Bess shot me a look. "You mean the stuff with Ibrahim on BetterLife? Do you really think that could be connected to all this?"

"Who knows? The timing is certainly interesting."

"Then there's only one thing to do," George said. "Go back online. See what's happening there, see if you can figure out who's controlling Guitarlvr15, maybe check into that UrNewReality character a little more, and then decide what to do."

I hated to admit it, but she was right. "All right," I said reluctantly. "I guess it wouldn't hurt to sniff around a little. Virtually speaking, that is."

Minutes later we were in George's bedroom, ensconced in front of the wall of computers on her desk. She always has half a dozen or so there, with several of them usually half taken apart.

With her obsession for technology and a limited budget, she's developed a talent for rebuilding computers and other gadgets that others have discarded.

"Thirty new messages since the last time we checked," she reported as she clicked through to BetterLife. "Including one from your new pal."

I leaned forward. The first three or four message headlines were the usual outraged textspeak drivel. But after that was a new one from UrNewReality with the subject line BREAKING NEWS. George clicked on it to reveal the message:

UNR IS WATCHING U
UNR KNOWS WHERE U GO & WHAT U DO
UNR HOPES U LEARNED SOMETHING @ SKOOL 2DAY

"Yikes," Bess said. "Kind of sounds like he knows you were just at the university, doesn't it?"

"Maybe, or maybe not," I said thoughtfully. "If this UrNewReality person thinks I'm just another middle schooler because that's where my avatar hangs out, it might be a random comment."

George looked doubtful. "In case you forgot, it's Saturday."

"Good point." I rubbed my chin and stared at the message. "I have to admit, this is more than a little suspicious."

"Not to mention creepy," Bess added.

Meanwhile George was already clicking out of my in-box and into the main game portal. Soon we were back at VirtualNancy's home. The virtual protest was still going on, though the numbers had thinned and Guitarlvr15 was nowhere in sight.

"I guess it's time to let VirtualNancy do some sleuthing," I said. "Let's bring her outside."

"Are you sure?" Bess's eyes widened. "But the protest . . . Some of these people seem really outraged."

I shrugged. "What are they going to do, virtually kill me?" I joked.

Soon VirtualNancy was stepping out her front door. As Bess had feared, several of the anti-VN protesters immediately raced over, shaking their virtual fists or waving their signs. A few of them started yelling at me, but George quickly blocked them. Their rants still appeared on-screen, but at least they couldn't harass me privately while blocked.

"Let's go talk to my supporters," I suggested. "Maybe one of them knows what's going on.

After all, there must be a reason they're supporting me, right?"

The pro-VN people clustered around as Virtual-Nancy approached. OMG! one avatar said, rushing over. She was a young teen girl with a Siamese cat on a leash. PEEPS R SOOOOOOO MEAN 2 U!!!!!I!!

THX, George typed on VirtualNancy's behalf.

Seeming satisfied, the girl and her cat wandered off. "Well, that was useful," Bess commented.

"Check it out, here's Ned," George said. "I would've thought he'd still be doing the Clark Kent thing over at the university."

"Maybe he just filed his story at one of the university computers and is checking in on BetterLife," I guessed.

However, I was a little surprised to see Ned-Nick02 in action at a time like this. Several of the other avatars, including the tall, blond MrNice-Guy I'd noticed earlier, were marching around in circles without changing their pattern or expression. I'd spent enough time on BetterLife by now to know that that meant they were on autopilot, so to speak—in other words, their creators had set them to keep doing what they were doing until they returned to control their next set of actions. But NedNick02 was definitely in "active" mode.

I leaned my elbows on George's desk to watch as NedNick02 approached, along with another avatar I'd noticed earlier, ParteeGrl21, the pretty young blond in the miniskirt. "Wonder if she's anyone we know?" I commented.

"Maybe it's Deirdre," George said with a snort. "She likes to show off her legs just like this chick obviously does."

I grinned. The three of us have known Deirdre Shannon since kindergarten. She's your basic dictionary definition of a spoiled little rich girl, and George, particularly, finds her insufferable.

"No way," Bess said. "Deirdre would never have a blond avatar. She once told me blond hair is, like, totally tacky." She patted her own blond tresses and smiled.

"The hair isn't the only thing tacky about that getup," George commented, taking in the avatar's go-go boots and plunging neckline.

On-screen, ParteeGrl21 addressed VirtualNancy. HI! she said with a smile. I'M PG21. IT'S NICE 2 FINALLY MEET U!

THX, VirtualNancy replied, thanks to George's flying fingers. IT'S NICE 2 C PEEPS STICKING UP 4 ME.

"Stop using those weird abbreviations," I complained. "I would never type that way—Ned will wonder if it's really me." I shoved her aside and took over the keyboard.

I'VE SEEN U HANGING AROUND LATELY, Partee-Grl21 was saying. U SEEM LIKE A FUN PERSON. O, & I LUV UR SENSE OF STYLE!!!

Bess beamed. "Okay, so maybe her outfit isn't exactly vintage Chanel," she said. "But the girl's obviously got taste!"

NE-WAY, ParteeGrl21 went on, I WUZ JUST GOING 2 ASK IF YOU WANTED 2 HANG AND B PALS WHEN U-KNO-WHUT HAPPENED. I KNO U DIDN'T DO IT!!!

REALLY? I typed. THANKS. BUT HOW COULD YOU TELL?

I HAVE GR8 INSTINCTS ABOUT PPL, she typed back. I WANTED 2 SUPPORT U.

Weird. How could some total stranger possibly know what I had or hadn't done? And what good were "instincts" in this bizarre online world, where people could make up any identity they wanted? Talk about gullible . . .

My new friend was still talking. I'VE BEEN ON BL SINCE BETA, she said. SO IF YOU NEED ANY HELP FINDING UR WAY AROUND . . .

"Beta?" I said aloud.

"The beta version of the game, I guess," George

said with a shrug. "That means she's been playing BetterLife for a long time."

"Hmm. Sounds like she could be a valuable friend to have on here, then," I commented.

Just then NedNick02 pushed his way forward. xoxo vn!!!! he said.

"That means hugs and kisses," George supplied.

"Even I know that!" I said.

Bess giggled. "Whoa, Ned's way more forward online than he is in real life!"

That much was true. Ned wasn't normally the "hugs and kisses" type. It seemed that hiding behind an online avatar was allowing his inner tween girl to emerge! It was sort of amusing, but I wasn't totally sure I liked it.

Luckily ParteeGrl21 didn't seem to mind the interruption. She and NedNick02 were already trading introductions. how do u kno vn? ParteeGrl21 asked.

lol—y don't u ask vn? NedNick02 replied. The avatar's expression changed to a teasing grin.

very funny, I typed.

ur not ashamed of me, r u? NedNick02 teased.

At least I hoped he was still just teasing. Given

our situation lately, I suddenly wasn't totally sure. OF COURSE NOT, I typed.

Y DON'T U PROVE IT BY GIVING ME A HUG? NedNick02 stepped closer to VirtualNancy and held up his arms.

"Wow. *Way* more forward," George said as she watched.

I was definitely feeling uncomfortable by now. But what could I do? I allowed NedNick02 to put his arms around VirtualNancy.

AWWW, 2 KYOOT! ParteeGrl21 said. DO U GUYZ KNO EACH OTHER IRL?

That was one abbreviation I didn't need my friends to translate; I already knew that "IRL" stood for "in real life." I was about to type in my reply when one of the anti-VN protesters suddenly rushed toward VirtualNancy and the others.

WE DON'T WANT UR TYPE HERE!!!!!1!!!1!!!! he shouted, raising his virtual fists. He was a big, beefy guy in a leather jacket with the handle KrazeeBiker.

I actually gasped out loud as I realized he was about to attack VirtualNancy. Okay, I know none of it was real. But it was still shocking to realize that someone could so suddenly turn violent, even online.

"Quick, have her duck!" George cried, reaching for the controls.

Before either she or I could do anything, NedNick02 flung himself in front of KrazeeBiker. LEAVE HER ALONE! he cried.

"Now *that's* more like the Dudley Do-Right Ned we know and love," Bess remarked.

Finding himself blocked, KrazeeBiker's expression changed to an irritated snarl. His fists were still up, and I expected him to hit NedNick02. Instead, he turned and punched ParteeGrl21 square in the face!

6

SPECIAL DELIVERY

ParteeGrl21 went down flat on the virtual ground, and a trickle of blood appeared under her nose. "Wow," George said admiringly. "The graphic effects just keep getting better and better on this site!"

I was much less concerned about that than I was about my new online pal. KrazeeBiker was already racing away with NedNick02 chasing after him. Meanwhile I sent VirtualNancy over to ParteeGrl21's prostrate form.

ARE YOU OKAY? I asked her. I'M SO SORRY!

DON'T WORRY, SWEETIE, she said as she sat up. I'M OK. IT WUD TAKE MORE THAN A JERK LIKE THAT 2 PUT ME OFF-LINE 4 GOOD!

I was relieved. But I still felt terrible for involving another innocent person in my problems, even virtually. ParteeGrl21 had been so nice that I wished I could tell her the truth about the whole crazy situation. But I held back. I could only imagine some entire real-life sorority house over at RHU being regaled with all the sordid details over dinner that night!

At that moment the doorbell chimed downstairs. "Rats," George said. "Nobody else is home—guess I'd better get that."

I hardly saw her go. SORRY, I typed as ParteeGrl21 stood up. I GUESS SOME PEOPLE THINK I REALLY DID WHAT THAT VIDEO SHOWS. BUT I PROMISE I DIDN'T.

THAT'S KOOL, ParteeGrl21 responded. I B-LIEVE U.

"Hey," George's voice floated up from downstairs. "Get down here, you guys."

EXCUSE ME, I typed hastily.

"You can abbreviate stuff like that, you know," Bess said as we both got up and hurried for the stairs. "Like you could use BRB for 'be right back,' or GTG for 'got to go.'"

"Whatever," I said. "Call me old-fashioned, but I prefer whole words."

When we reached the foyer, the front door

was open. A skinny college-aged guy was standing just outside balancing a large stack of white pizza boxes.

"One of you Nancy Drew?" he asked.

"I'm Nancy Drew," I replied.

"Great. Got your dozen extra-large anchovy pizzas right here." He took a step forward as if to shove his stack of boxes at me.

I took a step back. "Huh?" I said. "Sorry, but you must have the wrong house. We didn't order any pizzas."

The delivery guy frowned, looking irritated. "Yeah, that's what she said." He jerked a thumb in George's direction. "But I got the order slip right here. See?"

He balanced the boxes on one arm long enough to hand over a slip of slightly greasy paper. It not only had my name on it, but also George's address and my cell phone number.

Okay, *that* was weird. . . . "Look, I definitely didn't order these pizzas," I said firmly. "You'll have to take them back."

The delivery guy scowled. "I can't take them back," he said. "I'll get charged for these pies myself if I don't deliver 'em."

"Oh, but I'm sure your boss will understand if we call and explain," Bess said, tilting her head and shooting him her best smile and eyelash-flutter. No guy alive can resist that look for long. "I promise I'll have it taken care of by the time you get back there, okay?"

The guy hesitated, then finally shrugged. "Whatever," he muttered. "I'm not paying, that's all I can say." He turned and marched off toward the car parked at the curb.

Bess was already heading for the nearest phone. When she hung up a few minutes later, she grimaced. "The delivery guy is off the hook," she reported. "But Nancy, you probably shouldn't try to order from Sylvio's any time soon. They sounded pretty annoyed with your flip-flopping, especially since you supposedly made such a big deal about it being a huge rush order when you called a few minutes ago."

"But I didn't call!" I exclaimed. "I mean, I don't even like anchovies!"

"Duh," George said, drifting toward the stairs. "You know, the car thing might have been a coincidence. But now it's really starting to look like someone's out to cause you trouble—both online and in real life."

Back at George's computer, we found Partee-Grl21 repeating VN? VN? RU THERE? over and over again.

I hurried to the keyboard. SORRY, I typed I HAD TO STEP AWAY FOR A SEC. I hesitated, my fingers poised over the keys, once again wishing I could just tell her the truth. IT WAS SORT OF AN EMERGENCY.

O NO!!! she replied. R U OK??!?!

YES, FINE, I typed back. NOT THAT KIND OF EMERGENCY. JUST SOMEONE AT THE DOOR.

OK, she said. SRRY, DIDN'T MEAN 2 B NOSY. U DON'T HAVE 2 GIVE ME THE DEETS. IT'S SMART 2 B CAREFUL ONLINE UNTIL U FIGURE OUT WHO U CAN TRUST.

THANKS, I typed, still feeling vaguely guilty.

I KNO U WILL TRUST ME ONCE WE GET 2 KNO EACH OTHER BETTER, she continued. I'LL START BY TELLING U THAT IRL I'M A PREMED STUDENT. I GOOF OFF ON BL B/C I'M 2 BUSY STUDYING 2 HIT UP AS MANY PARTIES AS I WANT 2!

With that, the avatar made a funny little grimace. I smiled, touched that she was so willing to share more about herself. Still, I wasn't about to spill my guts to someone I'd just met, no matter how nice she seemed.

SO YOU'RE GOING TO BE A DOCTOR? THAT'S COOL, I typed instead. I BET YOU'LL BE GOOD AT IT—YOU'RE ALREADY MAKING ME FEEL BETTER!

The computer let out a beep. "New mail,"

George said, pointing to a blinking envelope icon in the corner. "Want to check it out?"

I clicked over and saw that it was another message from UrNewReality. The subject line read R U HUNGRY? and when I opened the text box all I found was a grinning smiley and the notation LOL!

"Whoa," Bess said. "Does that mean UrNew-Reality sent those pizzas?"

I was wondering exactly the same thing myself. "But how did he—or she, or they, or it, or whatever—know my cell phone number?" I exclaimed. "Let alone know that I was over at George's right now!"

George shrugged. "Anyone with the skills to hack into BetterLife can probably pull up all that info from the site's database—your phone number is listed in there, and I guess maybe they can track the origin of your current activity or something, too. So much for the BetterLife privacy agreement . . ."

I bit my lip, feeling increasingly uneasy. It was one thing to have bad guys after you in real life. With my history of crime solving, I was used to that. But this was different—and much weirder.

"It's getting late," I realized as the clock in the corner of the computer screen caught my eye. "I should probably check in at home before they think I've disappeared into the online world for good."

I typed a quick good-bye to ParteeGrl21 and logged off. Then Bess drove me home.

When I got there, I was just in time to meet Hannah Gruen on her way out. Hannah has been our live-in housekeeper ever since my mom died when I was little. She takes great care of Dad and me and is basically a member of the family.

"Oh, Nancy! There you are," she said, straightening her skirt. "I just left you a note on the fridge. I'm going out to dinner with friends, and your father is working late at the office on that new case of his. There's frozen pizza if you want to heat it up."

"Thanks." I bit back a grimace at the mention of pizza. "Have fun, Hannah."

Once inside, I checked the answering machine to see if the garage had called yet about my car. There were no new messages, so next I headed upstairs to check my e-mail and found a message from the head of my volunteer committee asking if I could work at the opening evening of Peace Week on Friday. Remembering that that was the night Ned and I had tentatively planned to go out, I wrote back quickly to let her know I couldn't make it and why, though I did confirm that I'd be at Monday's meeting. Then I logged off and wandered back downstairs.

Thinking about that date made me realize that Friday was way too far away. I didn't want to wait that long to get things back on track with Ned. On impulse, I reached for the phone in the kitchen. If Ned had time to mess around on BetterLife, maybe he'd have time to squeeze in that Saturday-night dinner we'd originally planned after all. . . .

I tried his cell phone number first, but it went straight to voice mail. Not bothering to leave a message, I tried again, this time dialing his home number.

"Hello, Nickerson residence," a familiar voice answered on the second ring.

"Ibrahim?" I said, a little surprised that he was answering the phone after what had happened earlier that day.

"Nancy!" He sounded delighted. "Oh, it is so good to hear from a friendly voice on a strange and difficult day like today!"

"Strange and difficult" seemed like an understatement. "How's everything going?" I asked. "How's Arij?"

"She is upset, but otherwise unharmed—perhaps

thanks to the quick-thinking woman who pushed
her aside and alerted us all to what was happening." Ibrahim's voice went uncharacteristically
somber. "It is still impossible for me to believe
that anyone would try to hurt my father by
harming Arij."

"Do the police have any leads yet?" I asked.

"I do not know." He sighed. "My parents will
not tell us anything. I know they are only trying to protect us, but still I cannot wait until
tomorrow when perhaps they will let me leave
the house again."

"Hang in there," I said, not sure what else to
say to make him feel better. "And remember you
have lots of friends in River Heights."

"Thank you, Nancy." He sounded grateful. "It
is good to know that indeed. Speaking of which,
is there a chance you might be able to meet me
for coffee again tomorrow?"

"Coffee? Tomorrow?" I repeated, taken by surprise.

"Coffee, or lunch, or anything you like," he
said. "Please? It can be my treat. I just would like
to go out and feel normal again after this weird
day."

"Oh." I chuckled sympathetically. "I hear you.
And of course, I'd be happy to hang out for a

little while. Should we say Barbara's Beans, around three?"

"Perfect!" he agreed, sounding more like his normal self already. "I look forward to it, Nancy."

"Great. Um, is Ned there? I was hoping to catch him."

"Of course. I'll get him."

I heard the clunk of the phone being set down. Tapping my foot, I waited. While I did, I thought about everything that had happened that day. It seemed like ages ago that I'd watched VirtualNancy chase Ibrahim's avatar down the streets of virtual River Heights. Unfortunately, I wasn't really any closer now to knowing who was behind it. And now there was this business with Professor al-Fulani to complicate things. . . .

"Nancy?" Ned's voice broke into my thoughts.

"Oh, hey! What's up? I was hoping you'd be home."

He cleared his throat. "Where else would a dull boy like me be on a Saturday night?"

I blinked, confused. Not only did his comment make little sense, but his voice sounded funny— stiff and oddly formal.

Suddenly remembering how weird he'd acted on BetterLife earlier, I wondered if this was part of his new NedNick02 schtick. "You're not still afraid I'm ashamed of you or whatever, are you?" I joked weakly. "I thought the hug cleared that up. Or the virtual hug, or whatever."

"Huh? What do you mean?" Now he was the one who sounded confused.

"Forget it." Suddenly I was really tired of all the online game-playing. "Listen, do you need to stick around at home tonight? If not, I was thinking maybe we could grab dinner tonight after all. Or dessert or something, if you've already eaten."

There was a very long pause. It was so long that if I hadn't been able to hear the Nickersons' TV playing the local news in the background, I would have wondered if we'd lost the connection.

"Look," he said at last, his voice strained. "You might want to check in on your 'better life,' then let me know if you really want to get together tonight. I'll talk to you later, okay?"

Before I could respond—or even figure out what he was talking about—he hung up. I stared at the phone in surprise. My "better life"? What was going on?

Hanging up, I hurried upstairs and logged on to the Internet again. Seconds later I was connected to BetterLife. When the welcome screen popped up, my own name caught my eye among the headlines on the community bulletin board. I blinked as I read the headline: I'M NANCY DREW: COME READ MY SECRET THOUGHTS!

"What?" I gasped, clicking on the headline to see more.

To my horror, I saw a series of e-mails start scrolling down the screen—*my* e-mails, basically all the ones I'd sent within the past couple of days. There was the one I'd just sent to the volunteer chairwoman explaining that I had a date on Friday night. A birthday message I'd sent to my cousin in Cleveland. One to Ned about our constantly changing plans. A handful of messages to Bess and George about this and that.

Then there was the last one on the list. It was addressed to Bess and George, but unlike the others, I knew right away that I hadn't sent it. But there it was, looking just as legit as the rest:

HEY GUYS,
NED MAKES ME WANT TO SCREAM SOMETIMES! HE'S JUST SOOOOOOO DULL!!! HE NEVER WANTS TO GO ANYWHERE DIFFERENT OR DO ANYTHING FUN. I'M STARTING TO THINK I CAN DEFINITELY DO BETTER.
LUV, NED NICKERSON'S SOON-TO-BE-EX GF,
NANCY DREW

7

DEAD ENDS AND DELAYS

When I walked into the kitchen the next morning, my father was sitting at the table with a plate of scrambled eggs in front of him. He looked up from the newspaper when I came in.

"Morning, Nancy," he said, stifling a yawn.

"Is that really you?" I joked, opening the refrigerator and grabbing a single-serving bottle of OJ. "You've been working so hard, I almost forgot what you look like."

"Sorry about that." He smiled sheepishly, setting aside the paper. "This case I'm working on is a monster."

"Anything you can talk about?"

He shook his head. "Sorry, can't," he said. "You know the drill. Supersensitive material, top secret info, yadda yadda. It's looking pretty touch and go whether we'll be able to get a conviction and make it stick."

"Got it." I leaned over to give him a kiss on the forehead. "Guess I'll have to read about it in the *Bugle* when it's all over, huh?"

"Something like that." He smiled. "Speaking of the *Bugle*, it sounds like there was some commotion over at the university yesterday. You hear about that?"

I glanced down at the newspaper. Sure enough, a headline halfway down the front page blared VISITING PROFESSOR THREATENED; POLICE CALLED AS PRESS CONFERENCE TURNS POTENTIALLY DEADLY.

"Yeah, as a matter of fact, I did," I said, picking up the paper and scanning the article. It didn't say much that I didn't already know. Along with photos of Professor al-Fulani, there was a shot of Shannon's aunt standing on the university green looking rather confused. The caption underneath read: LOCAL WOMAN AND FREQUENT CONTRIBUTOR TO OUR LETTERS TO THE EDITOR PAGE AGNES FITZGERALD IS BEING HAILED AS A HERO FOR HER QUICK THINKING AND IMMEDIATE ACTION.

"Sounds like the police assume it was all some kind of prank," my father said, reaching for his coffee. "Just someone causing trouble with one of those laser pointers."

"Yeah, that's what George said, too." I set down the paper. "Speaking of which, Bess should be here any second to drive me over to George's house. Have a good morning, and don't work too hard."

Dad grimaced. "Too late. Anyway, I'm off to the office as soon as I finish eating. When I surface from this case, how about a nice father-daughter dinner or something?"

"It's a date." I smiled and hurried out of the room.

Bess was just pulling to the curb as I stepped outside. "Did you talk to Ned?" she asked when I climbed in.

"Uh-huh. I called him right after I e-mailed you guys." I'd sent her and George the link to that bulletin board page as soon as the shock had worn off. "I'm pretty sure things are smoothed over—he knows I'd never write something like that about him; he just needed to hear me say it. And we're definitely going to talk things out more thoroughly on Friday's date, if not before." I sighed, popping open my OJ. "I'm not too worried about that. What I am worried about is figuring out who's targeting me and why."

Bess, George, and I spent the next couple of hours trying to do exactly that. However, we didn't make much progress. There were no new messages from UrNewReality, and most of the virtual protesters had disappeared from in front of VirtualNancy's home. Guitarlvr15 was nowhere to be found, and ParteeGrl21 and NedNick02 were both inactive. VirtualNancy wandered around for a while, garnering a few dirty looks and comments here and there, though most people seemed to have forgotten the scandal already and moved on to fresher gossip. Even so, George was still pushing for us to invent a new avatar for snooping around.

"No way," I told her when she brought it up for the third time. "One fake me is more than enough."

"Besides, VirtualNancy just got that hair-and-makeup upgrade, and we won't be able to take our custom-designed outfits with us to a new character," Bess added. "I'd hate to lose all our hard work!"

George rolled her eyes. "Whatever," she said.

"I'm hungry. Let's go scrounge up some lunch. Maybe you guys will see the light once you've eaten."

We were wolfing down the last bites of our peanut butter sandwiches when Hannah called to let me know the garage was looking for me. When I called the owner, Mr. Carr, he apologized for not yet having an answer on my car.

"We've been swamped this weekend, Nancy," he said. "We'll definitely take a look at it tomorrow. In the meantime, I can have the guys drop off a loaner car if you like. No charge."

"Thanks, that would be great," I said, telling him where I was. That was a relief—I'd been worried about how I was supposed to get over to River Street to meet Ibrahim in a couple of hours, since Bess and George were leaving for a family party in less than an hour and wouldn't be able to drive me around for the rest of the day. Now I wouldn't have to beg Hannah for a ride or take my bike.

I hung up and gave my friends the news. "At least that's one problem solved," I added. "Now if only we could get a handle on this case before this UrNewReality character decides to switch out all the songs on my iPod to elevator music or something. . . ."

"Impossible," George said. "Even the greatest hacker in the world couldn't do that." She paused, looking thoughtful. "At least I don't think so. But you might want to make sure it's unplugged just in case."

I sneaked a peek at my watch. It was just after five. I'd been sitting at Barbara's Beans chatting with Ibrahim for more than two hours. He'd seemed so happy and relieved to be out being "normal" again that I hadn't had the heart to cut our visit short, even though my half-finished cappuccino had gone cold long ago and the remainder of the foam had congealed into an unappetizing film at the top.

Oh, well. So much for stopping off at Sylvio's today, I thought. I'd hoped to visit the pizza parlor that day and ask around about the caller who'd ordered those pizzas in my name, but the restaurant closed early on Sundays.

Just then Ibrahim's cell phone rang. "Excuse me, Nancy," he said, picking it up. "Hello? Oh hi, Ned." He listened for a moment, then sighed. "Oh, I see. All right, I suppose Nancy will forgive me if I must rush off. . . . What? Yes, your Nancy. We're having coffee and a nice talk."

I winced. This certainly wasn't going to change

Ned's impression that I was spending too much time with Ibrahim!

"I'm afraid I must go," Ibrahim told me sadly when he hung up. "My father has asked me to be home early tonight. I know he is still worried about what happened yesterday."

"That's all right," I said, standing up. "I understand."

After he left, I checked my watch again—definitely too late for Sylvio's. Instead, I wandered over to the computers against the wall. The coffee shop wasn't very busy at the moment, and there were several open monitors. Sitting down at one, I logged on to BetterLife.

FIVE NEW MESSAGES, my welcome screen informed me. I clicked through them. Only three were hate mail this time. Another was a mass mailing about a sale at the virtual mall, and the last an administrative message from the site informing me that my job title had been upgraded. There was nothing at all from UrNewReality.

I sat there for a moment tapping my fingers on the computer table, wondering what to do next. Without George and Bess there helping me, hitting buttons to make VirtualNancy wander around seemed pointless and boring. Even more than usual, I mean.

A text box popped up on-screen. A FRIEND HAS INVITED YOU TO COME OUTSIDE, it read. At the bottom was ParteeGrl21's name.

I got VirtualNancy up and took her outside. Sure enough, a familiar miniskirted figure was waiting there.

HI VN, ParteeGrl21 greeted me. HOWZ IT GOING?

OKAY, I typed back. HOW ARE YOU?

A few picketers were still on the job nearby. One of them separated from the others and hurried toward us. It was NedNick02.

HI GRLZ, he said. HEY PG21, CAN I TALK 2 VN 4 A SEC?

TOTALLY, ParteeGrl21 replied with a wink icon. I'LL LEAVE U 2 LUVBIRDS ALONE. TTYL!

She walked away and disappeared off the edge of the screen. I stared at NedNick02, wondering if Ned had figured out from his conversation with Ibrahim that I'd be likely to check in on BetterLife at the coffee shop. He was smart that way.

HI, I greeted him. I'M GLAD YOU'RE HERE. IS EVERYTHING OKAY BETWEEN US?

TOTALLY, he typed back. HOW COULD I STAY MAD @ U?

I HOPE YOU BELIEVE I REALLY DIDN'T WRITE

THAT E-MAIL, I responded. I STILL FEEL BAD THAT
YOU GOT SUCKED INTO ALL THIS.

It felt pretty weird to be having this kind of
conversation online. Then again, why not? It had
been so hard lately for the two of us to get together
face-to-face—F2F, as George would have typed. I
might as well take what I could get.

I'LL ONLY 4GIVE YOU ON 1 CONDITION, Ned-
Nick02 said. U HAVE 2 GIVE ME A HUG.

Again with the hugging! Apparently being
"virtual" was making Ned bolder than he was in
real life. *Much* bolder.

Suddenly I felt an uneasy jolt of doubt. This
was Ned, wasn't it?

To make sure, I decided to give him a little
test. HEY, I typed quickly. DID I LEAVE MY LAPTOP
AT YOUR HOUSE?

That should do it, I thought as I hit the button
to send the text. If this was Ned, he would know
I didn't even own a laptop.

I DON'T WANT 2 TALK ABOUT LAPTOPS, the
reply came right away. & I WON'T SETTLE 4 AN
ONLINE HUG. I WANT 2 C U 4 REAL. MEET ME
WHERE WE HAD OUR LAST REAL DATE? U KNO—
PICNIC SPOT BY THE RIVER.

When I read that, I relaxed immediately.
Shortly before leaving on a trip to New York a

couple of weeks earlier, we'd had a picnic at a local park's scenic overlook. Nobody but Ned would know about that.

Thinking about that day made me just as eager to see him as he seemed to see me. I'LL BE THERE IN 20 MINUTES, I typed, quickly estimating how long it was likely to take me to get there.

CAN'T WAIT. CU SOON.

I smiled and moved the mouse, preparing to log off. Before I could do so, another avatar approached VirtualNancy and said hi. For a second I thought it was a stranger. Then I took a closer look and realized it was MrNiceGuy, the handsome blond avatar I'd noticed protesting in my favor the day before.

HI, I returned his greeting. I WAS JUST ON MY WAY OFF-LINE.

PLZ DON'T GO! MrNiceGuy said. I WAS HOP-ING TO TALK W/U!

SORRY, I said. MAYBE ANOTHER TIME.

The avatar's face formed a frown. OK, IF U INSIST, he said. I'LL B WAITING 4 U!

I hesitated, finding the comment vaguely threatening. Then I shook it off and logged out. I could worry about the online world later. Right now, I had a real-life boyfriend to meet, and I didn't want to be late.

Exactly twenty minutes later my loaner car was parked in the otherwise deserted gravel lot at the park, and I was pacing back and forth on the grassy bluff overlooking a picturesque bend in the river. Ned wasn't there yet, which was a little surprising. His house was only a ten-minute drive away, and he was always prompt.

While I waited, my mind wandered back to the case. I walked to the edge of the bluff and stared out over the high iron safety railing, pondering everything that had happened in the past couple of days. I still hadn't come up with any decent motives for someone to be harassing me, let alone a good suspect. Maybe George was right and I should consider whether Dad's case had anything to do with it.

Just then I heard a crunch of gravel from the direction of the parking lot. I spun around, expecting to see Ned.

Instead, I was just in time to spot a large rock flying straight at me!

8

MESSAGE RECEIVED

ducked just in time. The rock whizzed past my head, close enough for me to feel the slight breeze it made.

"Oh!" I cried, staring around wildly.

The sound of running footsteps snapped me out of my shock. Whoever had thrown the rock had been hiding behind my car! I gave chase, squinting against the fading daylight to try to identify exactly who it was I was chasing. But all I could see was a flash of dark fabric as whoever it was rounded a thick stand of trees between the parking lot and the next curve in the road. I put on a burst of speed, but before I could reach the trees I heard the roar of a car engine coming to life. By the time I made it around to get a view of the road, all that was visible was a cloud of dust disappearing around the curve.

I turned and dashed back to my loaner car. I'd left it unlocked with the key in the ignition, so all I had to do was jump in and turn the key. . . .

Click.

Instead of the sound of the engine coming to life, all I heard was a weak clicking sound. I tried again. Nothing. The car was dead!

I groaned, dropping my head against the steering wheel. Obviously, my attacker had made sure I wouldn't be able to follow. All I could do was listen helplessly to the last fading echoes of the other vehicle making its getaway.

I wish Bess was here, I thought. *Even if she couldn't get this car started quickly enough to go after him, she'd probably be able to ID the getaway car just by listening to it roar away.*

Realizing that such thoughts weren't going to help me now, I turned my focus to what had just happened. Had the rock thrower followed me from the coffee shop and seized the opportunity to attack? I shivered slightly at the thought, suddenly feeling very vulnerable sitting there all alone in a nonfunctional car in the darkening Sunday evening. . . .

I grabbed my cell phone (which the garage guys had returned when they'd brought the loaner car) and dialed Ned's cell. It went straight to voice mail, so I tried his home number.

"Ned's not here, Nancy," Mrs. Nickerson told me. "He and his father got a call about forty-five minutes ago to drive out to Farmingville and cover some big accident over there."

"Thanks. No message. I'll call him later." I bit my lip as I hung up and stared at the phone in my hand. Farmingville was a half-hour drive from River Heights. If Mrs. Nickerson's time estimation was accurate—and knowing her, it probably was—that meant Ned must have left almost immediately after he'd called Ibrahim. It also meant there was no way he'd been messing around on BetterLife half an hour ago when I'd made those plans with NedNick02. It seemed I'd been tricked!

I should have seen it earlier, I thought, giving myself a mental kick in the behind. *First the weird advances, then him not answering the laptop question . . .*

I sighed and rubbed my forehead. Trying to live half my life online was throwing off my sleuthing instincts, and I didn't like it.

Lifting the phone again, I punched in Bess's number, hoping she was back from her party by now. She was, and immediately agreed to come to my rescue.

"Just sit tight until I get there," she ordered. "And it wouldn't be a bad idea to lock the car doors. Just in case."

"I'll be here," I replied.

As soon as I hung up, I opened the door and climbed out of the car. No way was I sitting in a locked car when I could be doing some sleuthing. Besides, my attacker was long gone. If he or she came back, I'd hear the car in plenty of time to decide what to do.

I wandered around the park, trying to spot anything suspicious in the rapidly fading light. There were lots of footprints in the dirt at the edge of the parking lot, but that didn't tell me much. The park was a popular spot for hikers and sightseers as well as picnickers, and it had been a nice day.

Next I headed over to check out the spot where I'd been standing when the rock had come flying at me. For the first time, I noticed that the rock hadn't gone over the edge of the bluff as I'd assumed. It was wedged into the slats of the safety railing. And unless the weak light was playing tricks on my eyes, there was something scrawled on it in black marker!

I grabbed it with both hands, jerking it loose from the railing. When I lifted it up for a better look, I could read what it said: MYOB.

Not exactly obscure netspeak. Someone wanted me to mind my own business. Interesting . . .

By the time Bess arrived, I hadn't reached any new conclusions about my discovery. Still, I couldn't help feeling a teensy bit more optimistic than I had been before. Even after almost being knocked out, it was somehow comforting to have a real, solid, nonvirtual clue in hand!

"Amateur stuff," Bess declared as soon as she took a look at the car. "The fuel filter's yanked loose. Don't worry, I'll have this thing running again in a jiff."

She grabbed a few tools from her car and got to work under mine. Fortunately she'd had the foresight to change from whatever she'd worn to the party to jeans and a polo shirt—Bess's version of dressing down. While she was working, I filled her in on what had happened.

"Wow, you're lucky you turned around when you did," she said when I finished, sitting up and staring at me with wide, worried blue eyes. "What if that rock had hit you on the head? You might've been knocked right over the railing."

"I know." I shuddered at the thought. "It's one thing to have someone after VirtualNancy online, but this is getting a little too real."

Bess nodded. "It's weird how real life and online life are overlapping again. Just like with Shannon. I think you should be really careful until you figure out who's doing this."

"Don't worry. I plan to be." I flashed back to what ParteeGrl21 had told me once about being cautious about the information you gave out online. "In *both* worlds."

When I got home, Dad was still at the office and Hannah was engrossed in a TV show. "Want something to eat, Nancy?" she asked when I walked into the den to say hi.

"Maybe a little later. But don't worry, I'll get it myself." I left her to her show and went up to my room.

When I logged on to BetterLife, a message from UrNewReality was waiting for me. There was no subject line, and when I clicked to open it, I found only one line of text:

LUV LIFE GOT U DOWN?

A NEW SUSPECT?

The next morning I spent a couple of hours on BetterLife without discovering anything new. The place was slow—it was Monday, and most people were at school or work. NedNick02 was nowhere to be seen. When I did a search for him I also checked his online profile, a page where users could enter information about their avatars, but it was blank. MrNiceGuy, ParteeGrl21, and most of the other names I recognized were inactive as well. I did catch a brief glimpse of Guitarlvr15 when VirtualNancy wandered through the virtual mall, but he disappeared immediately and I wasn't able to find him again even with a search.

That was frustrating. But at this point, I wasn't sure my old pal Guitarlvr15 had anything to do with the case anymore. The one I needed to focus on was NedNick02. Who was he? George was still trying to hack the BetterLife system but she wasn't having any luck, so that seemed to be another dead end for the moment.

As I pondered the difficulties of online investigating, I realized I'd almost forgotten about one of my few real-life leads—Aunt Agnes. Only a couple of days had passed since my Prius was vandalized; maybe she would still recall any suspicious activity she might have seen. It was worth a try, anyway.

I was thinking about calling the university to see if Agnes was working that day, hoping to swing by the dining hall before my volunteer meeting, when the phone rang. It was the garage.

"We went over your vehicle with a fine-tooth comb, and you were right," Mr. Carr told me grimly. "There's no way the computer system went haywire on its own. It was definitely tampered with—and by someone who knew exactly what they were doing. We had to contact the company to figure out how to fix it! But it's all right now."

"Thanks, Mr. Carr," I said. "I'll be able to

swing by and pick it up on my way to a meeting, um . . ." I glanced at my watch. "Oh! Right now!" I exclaimed, realizing it was later than I'd realized. Time seemed to pass differently in BetterLife. . . .

Soon I was back in my own car on the way to my meeting. The volunteer group had a lot to do to prepare for International Peace Week, which was only a few days away now. I was too busy to think much about the case for the rest of the afternoon. In fact, by the time we finished it was too late to stop at Sylvio's or try to track down Aunt Agnes or do anything except head straight home for dinner.

The next few days were just as busy. Tuesday at breakfast, my father asked me if I had any spare time that day. "If so, I could really use your help at the office," he said. "One of the secretaries is out with the flu, the others are already swamped with this new case, and the last two people the temp agency sent over couldn't handle the pace and were more trouble than they were worth. I'm really sorry to ask, but all it would be is filing, returning some calls, things like that."

"Sure, Dad," I said immediately. He was looking so haggard and distracted that I wanted to do anything I could to help until his case was over, even if it meant I had less time to work on my own case. I'd planned to check in on BetterLife after breakfast and then visit Sylvio's and Aunt Agnes. But all that would have to wait.

"Need anything else right now?" I asked Helena Olney, my father's senior secretary.

"Thanks, Nancy. You've done such a good job these past few days that I think we're almost back under control," she replied with a smile, peering at me over the tops of her cat's-eyeglasses. "If you could just cover the phones while I run downstairs for an hour or so, I'd appreciate it."

"No problem."

It was Thursday afternoon. I'd spent all day Tuesday and Wednesday at my dad's office, and had agreed to come in again on Thursday. That morning had been just as busy as the previous two days. But finally things were slowing down, and my thoughts were starting to return to the mystery.

As soon as Helena left, I sat down at the reception desk and logged on to the computer. I'd been checking in on BetterLife whenever I had a chance, and had spent a few minutes there after dinner the previous two nights. George was also monitoring things at home and had promised to call if she saw anything suspicious. There had been one additional message from UrNewReality the day before, but all it had said was UNR IS STILL WATCHING U. Creepy, but not particularly helpful.

I'd checked around for NedNick02 every time I'd logged on, but he seemed to be lying low. I'd asked ParteeGrl21 to keep a lookout for him, telling her only that I suspected it was someone else posing as my real-life boyfriend. She'd promised to do so, and when I checked now there was a message from her in my in-box.

HAVEN'T SEEN U-KNO-WHO, it said. BUT PING ME—STH ELSE IS NQR.

I ran a search and soon located her at the virtual smoothie shop. WHAT'S UP? I had Virtual-Nancy ask her. GOT YOUR MESSAGE.

HI, VN! She seemed happy to see me, judging by the smile that appeared on the avatar's face. GOOD 2 C U. WANTED 2 WARN YOU. WAS AT YR CONDO THIS A.M. & A GUY THERE WUZ ASKING ABOUT U. I SAID I WUZ A PAL OF YRS & KNEW U WOULDN'T B AROUND MUCH 2DAY.

WHO WAS HE? I asked. IT WASN'T NEDNICK02? OR GUITARLVR15?

NO, she wrote back. HIS NAME IS MRNICEGUY.

My eyes widened as I remembered the good-looking but rather pushy blond avatar. YES, I'VE SEEN HIM AROUND, I wrote. DO YOU KNOW WHO HE IS?

NO, she replied. BUT I SAW HIM AGAIN JUST NOW. AS SOON AS I WENT 2 THE MALL HE TURNED UP & ASKED ME ABOUT U AGAIN.

THANKS FOR LETTING ME KNOW, I wrote. I'VE GOT TO GO. BUT I'LL CHECK IN WITH YOU AGAIN LATER.

C U! she replied.

I logged off, deep in thought. Now that I focused on MrNiceGuy, I realized he'd been lurking around in the margins of things since soon after that fake video had been posted. Did it mean anything? Was he connected to NedNick02 somehow, or was he just an overly friendly wannabe online pal like ParteeGrl21?

The phone rang, startling me out of my thoughts. I took care of the call, but as soon as I finished I dialed Ned's cell number. Something had been bugging me for the past few days, and I'd just realized what it was. Whoever had posed as Fake Ned had known about that picnic spot overlooking the river. Not even Bess and George knew about that date, and I was positive I'd never mentioned it in any e-mails that the culprit could have seen when hacking into my account. So how had he or she known about the overlook?

"Oh! Hi," Ned said when I reached him. "I was just heading into Econ class." Was I imagining things, or did he sound a little more aloof than normal? As far as I was concerned, our date the next night couldn't come soon enough!

"This won't take long," I said. "I just need to ask you something. Did you ever tell anyone else about that picnic spot where we went right before I left for New York?"

"You mean the overlook?" he said. "Funny you should ask that now. Actually I just mentioned it to this guy I know."

"What guy?" My heart jumped with anticipation. Was it really going to be this easy? "And why were you guys talking about it?"

"Just a guy from my English class; his name's Lyle," Ned replied. "He was looking for a romantic spot to take a new date, so I suggested that overlook and, um, told him how much you liked it. You know."

I clutched the phone more tightly against my ear. "When was this conversation?"

"Um . . ." Ned paused, clearly thinking back. He knows me well enough to realize I wouldn't be asking unless I wanted a specific answer. "It was this past Friday, I think. Yeah. Definitely Friday—Lyle and I had dinner together at the dining hall after class that day."

"Tell me about this guy Lyle," I said. "What's he like?"

"I dunno. Just a guy. He's in my English class, like I said, and I think he's pre-law. He plays tight end on the RHU football team—actually, if you saw yesterday's paper, he made the front page. MVP at Sunday's game."

"Sunday's game," I repeated. "Wait—you mean the RHU football game over in Indiana?" I vaguely remembered the guys at the garage talking about that when I'd stopped in to pick up my car on Monday.

"That's the one."

So much for my brand-new prime suspect. There was no way Lyle could be the person who'd lobbed that rock at me on Sunday. Not if he was off being MVP at a football game in another state at the same time. Still, this had to mean something—all I had to do was figure out what it was.

"Listen," I said to Ned, "can you ask him if he mentioned that picnic spot to anyone else after you guys talked about it? It has to do with my case. Could be important."

"Sure. I'll see him in class later. I can ask him then."

"Thanks." Another phone line had just lit up, and I remembered I was supposed to be working. "Listen, I'll let you get to class. Call me later."

"Will do."

"So your dad actually let you off the hook today, huh?" George said when she opened the door to let me in on Friday right after lunch. I'd spent the morning at another volunteer committee meeting, but now I was ready to throw myself back into my case.

I stepped inside. "Yeah. Is Bess here?"

"Upstairs."

Soon all three of us were sitting in front of George's computer. Being there again was giving me weird déjà vu flashes. It was becoming bizarrely difficult to keep track of what was real and what was virtual in this investigation.

"Any new leads, Nancy?" Bess asked as she watched me guide VirtualNancy toward the virtual mall.

"Sort of." I told both of them about Ned's acquaintance Lyle. "Obviously he's not Ned Nick Oh Two himself, but maybe he mentioned the park thing to whoever tried to bean me on

Sunday. He missed class yesterday, but Ned's going to ask him as soon as he tracks him down."

Bess pretended to pout. "I still can't believe you and Ned sneaked off for some romantic picnic at the overlook and didn't even tell us about it."

I didn't respond. VirtualNancy had just stepped into the mall, and suddenly a tall, blond guy was rushing toward her. It was MrNiceGuy.

HI! he said. I WAS WAITING 4U. WANT 2 HANG OUT?

"Who's that?" Bess peered over my shoulder at the screen. "Ooh, he's cute!"

"He's a two-dimensional batch of pixels on a screen," I reminded her. "Also, I think he might be stalking me. Er, stalking VirtualNancy. Maybe both of us."

"Hey," George said, taking a closer look. "I recognize that guy. He kept private messaging me when I was scouting around with VirtualNancy yesterday. Wanted to talk and hang out and stuff. I finally had to block him just to get him to leave me alone."

My jaw tightened. Enough was enough. My fingers flew over the keyboard. WHO ARE YOU? AND WHY ARE YOU STALKING ME?

"Nancy, wait!" Bess cried.

George groaned and smacked herself on the

forehead. "When will you learn, Nance?" she complained. "Every time you confront someone like that, you just end up blocked!"

Realizing she was right, I steeled myself for the inevitable blast of sound that meant the other user had blocked me from talking to him. But it didn't come.

I'M SORRY, NANCY! MrNiceGuy responded. I WAS JUST PLAYING AROUND—I DIDN'T MEAN 2 SCARE U!!! IT'S JUST ME—IBRAHIM!

ANSWERS AND QUESTIONS

"Ibrahim?" I exclaimed out loud, staring at the screen. A second later my cell phone rang. "I'm sorry, Nancy!" Ibrahim cried when I answered. "I didn't mean any harm."

"So it really is you?" I asked him, still stunned. "But I don't understand."

"It is silly, I know." He let out a loud sigh. "After what happened with my other avatar, I thought I might create a second one to use instead—you know, until things cooled down. Besides, I thought it might give me the chance to hang out with you more, especially if I made the new avatar the type of guy you might like. I was on BetterLife during study hall just now and saw you log on, so I thought I'd say hi."

I stared at MrNiceGuy, who was still frozen on the computer screen. He was the physical opposite of Ibrahim in almost every way. What had made Ibrahim assume I went for the tall, blond, hunky, and aggressive type, anyway? It was more than a little icky to think about him pondering such things, and I couldn't help wondering if there was more to this than he was telling me. Could he possibly be involved with the rest of the mystery? After all, he knew Ned as well as anyone—well enough to fake being him online, perhaps . . . ?

But I quickly realized Ibrahim couldn't possibly be the culprit. For one thing, he'd been with me when that first message from UrNewReality had popped up in my in-box. Even if he'd been able to arrange that somehow, there was no way he could have sabotaged my car or pointed that laser at his sister or tossed that rock at me. And as much as I might be doubting my own abilities when it came to sleuthing online, in the real world I still trusted my instincts. And they were telling me that Ibrahim was exactly what he seemed—an innocent kid who'd made a mistake and was now owning up to it.

"It's okay, Ibrahim," I said. "No harm done.

I'm sorry for overreacting. It's just with everything that's been happening . . ."

"No, no, please, Nancy," he said earnestly. "It is me who is sorry! I should have thought more clearly about how this could seem to you."

I said good-bye and hung up, then told Bess and George what Ibrahim had said. "We should have guessed," George commented. "After all, there's a thin line between trailing around after someone like a lovesick puppy and online stalking."

"Oh, come on. He's not that bad."

"Face it, Nancy," Bess put in. "The kid is head over heels. I know you can be a little clueless about these things, but even you have to see it!"

The conversation was definitely taking an uncomfortable turn. And more important, a pointless one.

"Never mind that," I said briskly, sticking my phone back in my pocket and turning toward the keyboard again. "Now that we know Mr. Nice Guy's not connected to the case—"

"We do?" George interrupted. "Are you sure about that? What if Ibrahim set up that whole attack on his avatar as a twisted way to get closer to you? He's pretty good with computers, right?"

"Not that good," I said. "Anyway, he definitely

didn't do most of the bad stuff that's been happening. He didn't have the opportunity. Like the rock at the overlook, for instance—he was at Ned's house under the watchful eyes of his parents at the time that was happening."

Bess nodded. "Good point. Anyway, I can't believe he'd do anything like that. He's a sweet person."

"Now that that's settled, let's move on." I stared at the computer screen, where MrNice-Guy had just winked out of existence. I guessed Ibrahim's study hall was over. "At least we've got one red herring out of the way. So let's focus on our other suspects."

"You mean that NedNick guy and Guitar-lvr15?" Bess asked.

I shrugged. "I was thinking more of the real-life person behind the avatar," I said. "It's starting to feel kind of ridiculous to go chasing all these fake people around a fake world."

"But that's kind of the point," George argued. "Whoever is doing this obviously has mad computer skills."

"Yeah, but that doesn't really narrow things down much." I shrugged. "I mean, most people these days have at least some level of computer competence, right?"

George smirked. "You mean aside from you?"

"Very funny." I rolled my eyes. "Anyway, it's almost impossible to tell who might have the additional skills to pull off some of these stunts. And unless and until we find a way into the BetterLife system ourselves, we won't be able to track down who's behind the avatars that way."

"So what are you saying—that this case is hopeless?" Bess sounded surprised.

"Maybe," I said. "At least if you're talking about solving it online. Our culprit is just too computer savvy—he or she isn't likely to slip up there, at least not in any way we're capable of catching." I shrugged. "But in the real world? That's another story."

"I think I see what you mean." Bess leaned on the computer desk and twirled one strand of blond hair around her finger. "The bad guy's been a little sloppy there. Taking risks—like tampering with your car in front of Shannon's house where anyone could happen past and see. Same with messing up the loaner car and throwing that rock."

George nodded, finally catching on. "Or making that call to the pizza place," she added. "What if the person on the other end knew Nancy's real voice and realized something was up?"

I sat up straight. "I almost forgot about that. I've been meaning to stop by Sylvio's and talk to whoever took that call. I just haven't quite made it happen yet." I made a face, realizing just how long I'd let it slide. "Living half online is really getting to me! My computer skills may be improving—"

"They are?" George put in dubiously.

"But my detective skills are slipping," I finished, ignoring her comment. Standing up, I headed for the door. "Come on, let's go. If we hurry, we can make it to Sylvio's before the dinner rush."

"Sorry." The portly middle-aged man behind the counter at Sylvio's scratched his half-bald head and shrugged. "We're always busy here, especially Saturdays. I mean, yeah, sure, I remember the call. All of us do—it was a weird order, you know? What with the big rush and the extra anchovies and everything . . ." He narrowed his eyes slightly and stared at me, as if still not fully convinced I hadn't been behind the mix-up somehow. A few of the other employees had been shooting me similar looks ever since my friends and I had entered and explained why we were there.

I sighed. "Are you sure you don't remember

anything more? Like, was it definitely a female voice who called?"

The man looked slightly insulted. "Well, sure, I can confirm that for you, miss," he said. "What, you think I'm not gonna remember a dude named Nancy?"

"But you're not sure whether the voice sounded like mine?" I pressed him.

He shrugged again. "Coulda sounded like you, I suppose," he said. "Then again, it was loud in here. Who knows?"

"Joey!" someone barked from back in the kitchen. "Call Anthony. He forgot the garlic bread for that birthday party delivery!"

"Got it," the man called back. He hurried off toward the phone at the other end of the counter without sparing me another glance.

"Oh, well," Bess said as the three of us wandered toward the exit. "At least that narrows things down a little. It means our culprit is female, right?"

"Maybe." I bit my lip. "Or it could just mean he knows a woman he talked into making that call. Or it could mean there's more than one person involved."

"So basically, we've still got nothing?" George asked.

I shrugged. "We've still got Aunt Agnes. The university dining hall is right down the street—let's see if she's working today."

She wasn't. The harried kid we asked didn't know when she'd be in next, either. Maybe dinner shift, maybe not . . .

"Now what?" George asked when we found ourselves back in my car again.

"We could try going to her house," Bess said. "Do you know where she lives, Nancy?"

I shook my head. "We could stop somewhere and check the phone book."

"We can do better than that," George said. "Let's stop at the coffee shop and look it up online."

Soon we were clustered in front of a monitor at Barbara's Beans. But no matter what she tried, George couldn't seem to turn up an address or phone number under the name Agnes Fitzgerald anywhere in the county.

"Weird," Bess said. "Do you think she lives really far away?"

"And commutes to a job as a dining hall worker?" George shook her head. "Doubtful. She's probably just unlisted—maybe she's a renter or something." She reached for the mouse. "Anyway, as long as we're here we might as well check in on BetterLife, right?"

I sighed. "I suppose so."

"Here we go," George said a second later as she clicked through to the site. "Another message from your secret not-so admirer!"

Sure enough, there was a new e-mail from UrNewReality in my in-box. This one read:

WHAT R U DOING 2 NIGHT, NANCY? UNR WILL B THERE 2!

"Yikes!" Bess exclaimed when she read it. "Extra creepy! Is he saying he's going to be spying on your date tonight?"

"Sounds like it, doesn't it? Good thing Ned will be right there with you, Nancy," George said. "Still, you'd better be careful—stay in well-lit public places, that kind of thing."

With a jolt, I realized I'd almost forgotten tonight's date. I checked my watch and saw that it was already past five o'clock. Once again, I realized I was sitting in front of a computer when I should be out investigating.

"You know, we're forgetting the obvious—we could just call Shannon's mom for Agnes's address or phone number," I said. "But it might have to be tomorrow. Unless you think Ned won't mind me showing up for our date looking like this?"

"No way!" Bess looked horrified as she took in the sight of me in my jeans, sneakers, and loose ponytail. "The case has waited this long; it can wait another day. Let's get you home and looking decent."

Normally I might have argued with her. Ned wasn't the type of guy who cared about clothes or makeup or anything like that. But this date was different. I really wanted to make up for all the canceled plans and misunderstandings lately, and remind him that I still thought he was special. It would be nice to put everything else out of my mind for a few hours and just enjoy being with him and reconnecting.

Besides, what are the odds Agnes will have seen anything, or will remember it a week later even if she did? I thought with a flash of pessimism. I could hardly believe how sloppy I'd been about following up my real-life leads. Somehow, I'd been so caught up in the online part that everything I knew about sleuthing had flown out the window.

We logged off and hurried back to my house. "Okay, first of all, what are you going to wear?" Bess asked when we reached my room.

"Hadn't really thought about it," I admitted.

At Bess's groan, George laughed. "I'm going to check in on BetterLife again while you guys are primping," she said, heading for my computer.

Bess was already rushing over to dig into my closet. "Here, this should do," she said, emerging seconds later with a dress I hadn't even remembered I owned. "Jump in the shower and then put it on, and after that we can talk about your hair."

She bustled around, her arms a blur as she grabbed hairbrush, makeup, accessories. . . . A short while later I was showered and changed. As Bess spritzed me with some cologne, George glanced up from the computer.

"Ah, looks like you've earned the perfume upgrade, Nance," she joked. "If you keep it up, you'll be almost as tricked out as your virtual half."

"Ha-ha," I said, sticking out my tongue at her. "So what are you guys doing tonight while I'm out with Ned?"

"I'm half tempted to tag along and spy on you," Bess admitted as she expertly twirled my hair around a brush. "What if UrNewReality tries something?"

"They'll be fine." George leaned back from the desk, both hands behind her head. "Actually, I wouldn't mind catching a movie or something."

"We can see a movie anytime," Bess said. "If we're not playing bodyguard, we really ought to go hear Professor al-Fulani's speech."

"I almost forgot that was tonight!" I said. "Maybe I should see if Ned wants to go see it before we eat. It should be a great speech."

Bess frowned. "Doesn't sound too romantic. Now, do you have any shoes that go with that dress?"

I shrugged. "Depends on your definition of 'go with' I suppose."

"Uh-oh," George put in. "Better hope your shoe upgrade comes through before you have to leave, Nancy."

"Not much chance of that." I checked my watch. "Ned will be here in, like, five minutes."

My cell phone rang. I'd tossed it on my bed as we came in, so I strode over and grabbed it. "Probably Ned saying he's running late or something," George said.

"Let's hope," Bess muttered from inside my closet, where she was digging through my modest shoe collection. "I could use a few extra minutes here."

"Hi," I said into the phone. "You on your way?"

"Er, Nancy?" a woman's voice said.

Not Ned. Oops.

"Oh, sorry—Mrs. Mahoney?" I said, recognizing the thin, reedy voice. The wealthy widow and philanthropist was cochair of the committee running Peace Week. "Is that you?"

"Where are you, Nancy?" Mrs. Mahoney was normally pretty unflappable. But at the moment she sounded downright flapped. "The children are all here, and I have to leave to go get ready to introduce the professor soon!"

"Huh?" I had no idea what she was talking about. Switching the phone to my other ear, I said, "Are you okay, Mrs. Mahoney? I'm just about to go out to dinner, but if you're shorthanded or something maybe Bess or George could—"

Mrs. Mahoney interrupted before I could finish, sounding more frantic than ever, plus slightly irritated. "What are you talking about, Nancy?" she cried. "You promised me you'd babysit during the speech tonight!"

UNEXPECTED DANGERS

gasped. Naturally, I knew right away that I'd made no such promise. I might be a little scatterbrained at times, but I'd never forget something like that.

"Wait," I said. "You mean you thought I was showing up to the professor's speech tonight to, um, *babysit*?"

"Of course! We exchanged several e-mails about it," Mrs. Mahoney said. "The latest one just this morning! You said you'd be here by six thirty with three or four friends." She sounded more irritated than ever now. "It was all your idea! You said we could raise additional money for the Peace Week charity by offering babysitting services to parents at a bargain price. And let me tell you, the parents out there are eager to take advantage of it! There must be twenty kids out there already, with more arriving all the time and nobody at all available to watch them!"

My heart sank. I was already certain that UrNewReality was behind this. He or she must have hacked into my account again and convinced Mrs. Mahoney it was me on the other end of those e-mails, the same way s/he'd convinced the pizza place it was me placing that order.

Unfortunately, this prank wasn't going to be as easy to resolve as that one. "I'm so sorry," I said into the phone. "Um, I'll be there as quickly as I can."

When I hung up, Bess and George were staring at me in confusion. "What was that all about?"

"No time to explain." I was already peeling off my dress and reaching for the jeans and T-shirt I'd dropped on the floor. "But the good news is, you guys don't have to wonder anymore about what you're doing tonight."

"Huh?" George said at the same time Bess cried, "Nancy! Why are you changing? And watch the hair!"

Also at the same moment, the doorbell rang downstairs. I groaned. "Oh, man," I muttered. "I am so *not* looking forward to explaining this to Ned. . . ."

Less than twenty minutes later, all four of us were at the university library in full babysitting mode. Ned had agreed to pitch in without complaint, just as I'd known he would. Still, I could tell he wasn't thrilled about having our date put off yet again. I knew just how he felt.

Luckily Bess likes kids and babysitting, so she was okay with the sudden change of plans, though George had been grumbling from the start. Our charges ranged in age from infants to middle schoolers. Keeping them from totally destroying the library kept us pretty busy, but even while kid-wrangling I was able to ponder the case a little. It was obvious that UrNewReality wasn't letting up on me. What was he or she after, anyway?

"Heads up!" Ned called from across the area where we were attempting to keep the kids contained, which lay between the librarian's desk and the open space scattered with study tables at the front of the library. "We've got a runaway!"

"I'm on it," I called back, spotting four-year-old Owen Zucker careening toward the copy machine at the edge of the seating area. Owen lived a few blocks from me, and I knew he could be a handful. I raced after him, catching him just before he crashed into the glass expanse of one of the floor-to-ceiling windows that lined the front wall of the library. "Gotcha!" I cried, grabbing him around the waist and tickling him.

As he shrieked and giggled, I glanced out the window. The college green was well-lit, offering a clear view of the picketers gathered outside the hall where the speech was taking place. Most of the protesters were marching in sort of a ragged circle, waving their signs and presumably chanting, though I couldn't hear them from inside the library. Their numbers had swelled since I'd passed them on the way in, and I was surprised to see a familiar figure among the newcomers.

Letting Owen wriggle loose and run back toward the others, I stepped closer to the window. *Is that Agnes Fitzgerald?* I wondered, peering at the heavyset, dark-haired figure standing at the edge of the marchers. It was hard to tell whether she was participating in the protest or just watching, perhaps on her way to or from her job at the dining hall.

Before I could figure it out, I heard a crash and a shriek. Wincing, I turned and saw a tipped-over chair and a red-faced little girl standing beside it, bawling. Bess was already comforting the girl and I headed that way to help. Halfway there, George intercepted me.

"Nancy, check it out," she said, holding up her cell phone. "I just got this e-mail."

"If this is some lame fake excuse to get out of babysitting, like saying your house is on fire or something, don't even bother," I joked, most of my attention still on the crying girl.

"No, listen." George grabbed me by the arm. "This is important."

When I glanced at her, I saw that her face was pale. "What is it?" I asked.

By way of answer, she shoved the phone toward me. I saw that it was in e-mail mode. A message was open, with the return address UrNew-Reality at the top. I quickly scanned the text:

TELL UR FRIEND NANCY DREW SHE'S NOT THE ONLY I WHO KNOWS HOW 2 SPY ON PEEPS. THERE R LOTS OF WINDOWS IN THE LIBRARY. . . .

I gasped, instantly flashing back to that creepy laser mark that Agnes had spotted on Arij's face. "Oh, my gosh," I exclaimed, my gaze shooting back to those front windows, which suddenly looked enormous and hopelessly fragile. "Are you thinking what I'm thinking?"

"Are you thinking this e-mail sounds like a

threat?" George asked grimly. "If so, then yeah."

"I can't let my crazy stalker put these kids in danger." I took a deep breath. "How do you make an outgoing call on this thing? Because I think we'd better call in the experts before things get out of control."

I figured Chief McGinnis would be attending the speech, and I was right. At first he wasn't thrilled about being interrupted, but he agreed to come and check things out. After hearing the whole story he still seemed dubious, but ordered a couple of his men to stand guard outside and advised us to keep the kids away from the windows.

"Keep them away from the windows?" George said, eyeing the floor-to-ceiling glass as the chief hurried out. "What are we supposed to do, make them lie on the floor for the next hour?"

"Fat chance," Ned put in breathlessly, trying to hang on to a pair of toddlers who were trying to pummel each other.

"I've got an idea," Bess said. Switching into her "kid voice," she singsonged, "Who wants to play hide-and-seek?"

For the rest of the evening, we played back in the stacks, which started behind the desk, well out of range of the big front windows. The kids loved it, and hiding and chasing kept them busy enough that only a few books got pulled off the shelves and/or drooled on. Still, I couldn't relax until the speech and reception were over and every last kid was safely back with his or her parents.

"Whew," I said, collapsing against a table as I watched Owen Zucker's parents drag him, still wriggling, out the door. "Glad that's over."

Ned wandered over. "Yeah, you sure know how to show a guy a good time," he joked, giving me a squeeze around the shoulders. "Want to try to salvage the rest of this so-called date? Maybe a late-night ice-cream run or something?"

I hated to put him off yet again. But I knew I'd never be able to focus on reconnecting now. I needed some time alone to process everything that had happened that evening and figure out what to do about it.

"Can I take a rain check on that?" I said reluctantly. "I'm beat."

"Sure." He dropped his arm and checked his watch. "You're right, it was probably a bad idea—it's getting pretty late."

Bess's car was still at my house from earlier, so Ned dropped all three of us there. "Come on, George," Bess said, digging into her purse for her keys. "This train's leaving the station in thirty seconds whether you're on board or not."

"Okay, coming." George reached into her pocket as her phone let out a beep. She glanced at it, then gasped. "Hey, look—it's UrNewReality again!"

"Oh, man," I moaned. "Doesn't this person ever sleep?"

"Maybe it really is an avatar," George said. "Computer-generated two-dimensional humanoids don't require sleep."

"Stop talking like that; you're making my head hurt," Bess complained. "What does the message say?"

George stepped over beneath the front porch light with Bess and me on either side. I squinted at the tiny letters on the phone's screen.

SHOULDN'T U CHECK ON UR BETTER HALF? UNR SAW HIM WATCHING U.

"Ned!" I blurted out, instantly flashing to a variety of horrible scenarios. UrNewReality seemed to like messing with cars; what if s/he had done something to Ned's while we were all in the library?

George was already dialing the phone. "Ned?" she said when he picked up. "Hey, there's been a new development. . . ." She handed the phone off to me so I could explain.

"I'm almost home, and everything's okay," he said. "I'll let you know if anything happens."

"Be careful," I told him, then hung up.

Bess was biting her lip. "I just had a thought," she said. "What if that message doesn't mean Ned after all? *Real* Ned, I mean."

I caught her drift immediately. "NedNick02," I said, hoping she was right. "You could be onto something—let's check it out."

My father was still at the office, and Hannah was in her room watching TV, so we hurried straight upstairs and logged on to BetterLife. It took only seconds to find NedNick02. He was lurking around outside VirtualNancy's home.

"Don't let him see you," Bess whispered, as if the avatar might hear her through the computer screen.

I nodded, keeping VirtualNancy out of sight behind some shrubbery. It was nighttime in Virtual River Heights, just like in the real one, and there were only a few people on the street—a group of chattering partiers, a couple of vampires, a boy walking his giraffe. Okay, so maybe Virtual River Heights wasn't *just* like the real thing. . . .

"Now what?" George mumbled, stifling a yawn. "Are we just going to sit around watching this dork stand there all night, or what?"

"Look, there he goes!" Bess cried.

Indeed, NedNick02 had just turned abruptly and walked off down the street. "Let's follow him," I said.

"Want me to take over?" George asked, sounding slightly more awake. "I know you're the expert at this sort of thing in real life, Nancy, but on the computer . . ."

"That's okay, I've got it." I was already directing VirtualNancy down the street after the other avatar. "Looks like he's heading downtown."

Soon we were in the virtual business district of the virtual town, which had a much livelier and more varied nightlife than the real thing. For instance, there was a traveling circus parked on the edge of the university campus that was doing a booming business. Several nightclubs were pulsing with loud dance music. There were also private parties at some of the homes in this part of town, including the enormous four-story ultramodern blue-and-purple turreted mansion that someone had built in the middle of State Avenue.

"Check it out—looks like he's looking to party," George said as NedNick02 turned up the jewel-encrusted front walk of the virtual mansion, paused to speak to the beefy avatar guarding the door, and then disappeared inside. "We might not be able to follow him any farther if we're not invited."

"All we can do is try," I said, marching Virtual-Nancy up to the bouncer.

R U ON THE LIST? the bouncer asked.

I JUST NEED TO GO INSIDE FOR A MINUTE, I responded. I HAVE TO TALK TO SOMEONE.

"Make her smile," Bess advised.

"What?"

"Smile," she repeated. "VirtualNancy's cute. That might make a difference with this guy."

I was skeptical, but did as she said. Before I could stop her, Bess leaned over and typed in UR CUTE. WANT 2 DANCE L8R?

"Hey!" I protested as Bess smirked.

SURE, the bouncer replied. GO ON IN. CATCH U L8R, QT!

"See?" Bess said proudly as VirtualNancy headed into the mansion. "Now do you two agree that all those hair and wardrobe upgrades weren't a waste of time?"

George rolled her eyes. "Whatever. How are we ever going to find that NedNick guy again in this huge place?"

"There he is," I said, spying him standing at

the foot of an elaborate curved marble staircase. "Looks like he's heading up."

I sent VirtualNancy after him, dodging the hundreds of others who were at the party. We made our way up one flight of stairs, down a hall, and then up another story.

"This place is nuts," George commented as we passed yet another room of partiers. The mansion seemed to have a different theme for every room, from ancient Rome to jungle safari to North Pole Christmas to Arabian Nights to American frontier. It really *was* nuts. But NedNick02 wasn't paying much attention to any of it, and neither was I.

We went up two more floors and finally wound up in a sort of greenhouse area with a spiral staircase leading up to the roof. NedNick02 headed straight for the staircase.

"Follow him!" George urged, leaning forward.

"What does it look like I'm doing?" I sent VirtualNancy up the stairs. She emerged a moment later onto the mansion's large, flat rooftop. There were a few partygoers up there, but it was easy to spot NedNick02. He was standing by himself at the edge of the roof a short distance away, staring out over the flickering lights of Virtual River Heights.

I marched VirtualNancy over to him and tapped him on the shoulder. "Careful, Nancy," Bess said. "What are you—"

WHO ARE YOU? I demanded.

George groaned. "Don't you ever learn?" she cried. "Are you *trying* to get yourself blocked?"

"No. But I'm tired of playing games," I said. "If UrNewReality wanted us to check this guy out, he could be . . ."

My voice trailed off as words began appearing in NedNick02's text box. DIDN'T ANYI EVER TELL U 2 MYOB?

"What's that supposed to—" George began.

I gasped, hardly hearing her. NedNick02 had just stepped behind VirtualNancy and given her a hard shove. "No!" I cried as she went flying— right over the edge of the roof!

The screen suddenly went black. A moment later a skull and crossbones floated into view:

WE'RE SORRY. GAME OVER.

A QUESTION OF CHARACTER

"Oh, my gosh!" Bess exclaimed. "Does this mean—is VirtualNancy—is she, you know, *dead*?"

I couldn't answer for a second. It was surprising just how shocking it felt to have my virtual self "killed" that way. "I—I didn't even know that could happen," I stammered at last, staring at the floating skull and crossbones.

"I did," George said. "I just never thought it would happen to us. To her. You know."

The death screen blinked out, replaced by a new one with a green background. It was an instruction screen that explained that we were welcome to re-create our avatar or build a brand-new one, but that we would have to start the game over again from scratch, with a new entry-level job, a cheap apartment, etc. THERE ARE NO DO-OVERS IN BETTERLIFE, the screen said. AS THEY SAY, YOU CAN'T TAKE IT WITH YOU.

"So we lost all our upgrades?" Bess sounded horrified. "This is terrible! After all the hard work I did on her hair, her makeup, her clothes . . . all for nothing!"

"Anybody home?" a voice drifted up from downstairs. It was my father.

We hurried down to say hello. Dad still looked exhausted, but there was a twinkle in his eye and a spring in his step that had been missing lately.

"You look chipper for a guy who just put in, like, fifteen hours at the office," I said, standing on tiptoe to give him a kiss on the cheek.

He grinned at me. "That's because we're getting close to settling this thing," he said, flinging his jacket on a chair and loosening his tie. "If nothing throws a wrench into the works, we may be able to wrap it up sometime next week."

"Congrats, Mr. D.," George said. Then she yawned and glanced at me and Bess. "It's pretty late. How about we call it a night and tackle our own wrench in the works in the morning?"

◆ ◆ ◆

"Okay," George said, bending over her computer keyboard. It was the next day, and we were getting ready to create a new avatar. "So we want this VirtualNancy to be totally different from the previous one, right?"

Bess nodded. "Right. But I don't think we should call it VirtualNancy."

"Duh." George hit a key to call up the BUILD YOUR AVATAR screen. "Let's put something together and then think of a good name."

"Sounds like a plan," I said weakly. I knew they were right—if we wanted to snoop around BetterLife on the down-low, our new avatar should be as different from dear departed VirtualNancy as possible. Besides, I knew lots of people created avatars that were very different from themselves for various reasons—like Ibrahim with MrNiceGuy, for instance, or Rebecca with Guitarlvr15. But I still felt a little weird about it. I'd never really wanted to be anyone other than myself.

George glanced over and caught my expression. "Think of it as going undercover," she advised. "By the way, I'm also fudging our member info this time in case UrNewReality is watching for a new 'Nancy' to pop up." She shrugged. "It might not help with a super-hacker like this, but at least maybe it'll buy us a little time."

"Okay." Bess rubbed her hands together. "So let's go—what would be the exact opposite of Nancy?"

"To start with, let's make her a boy." George hit a button, and a bland-looking blond guy appeared on the screen.

"No more blonds," Bess advised. "Let's give him dark hair."

"What style?" George's hand paused above the mouse.

"Guys, let's not get carried away here . . . ," I began.

But it was no use. Before I knew it, the two of them had created a super-fashionable male club kid with a faux-hawk. He had a pierced nose, tanned skin, guy-liner, and wildly cool clothes— or at least as cool as Bess could manage with a starter avatar's points.

"As soon as we get a couple of upgrades, maybe we can give him a gold tooth or something," Bess commented.

"What should we call him?" George asked.

"Keep it simple," I said. "How about something like CoolJoe or FunFred?"

"I know!" Bess didn't even bother to acknowledge my suggestions. "How about Dancin' Four Evah?"

"Perfect! Let's see if it's available." George typed it in, and there was a soft *ding*, indicating that the name had been accepted.

I sighed. "Okay, it was weird enough messing around, living a two-dimensional extra life with an avatar that at least resembled me. But with this creature . . ."

"Quit complaining," George advised. "Dancin-4Evah is the perfect cover. Nobody would *ever* guess he was yours!"

I had to agree with that. Soon Dancin4Evah was sniffing around Virtual River Heights looking for anything suspicious. But not much was happening at the moment.

"Too early, I guess," George said.

"Uh-huh. Maybe we should give up for now and—Hold that thought," I interrupted myself as my cell phone rang.

It was Ned. He was calling to say that he and his parents were having lunch with Professor al-Fulani and his family over at the university dining hall to celebrate how well last night's speech had gone, and my friends and I were invited to join them.

"We'll be there," I told him, deciding that lunch in the real world sounded a lot better than wasting any more time in the virtual world.

An hour later Bess, George, and I were walking across campus toward the dining hall. It was a pleasant Saturday afternoon and lots of students were out on the green studying, tossing Frisbees, or just hanging out.

"I wonder if Agnes Fitzgerald is working today," I said as we headed up the dining hall steps. "I'd still like to talk to her about last Saturday—see if she noticed anything."

"Who?" George said. "Oh, wait. You mean Shannon's Aunt Congeniality, right?"

"Uh-huh."

I glanced around as we went inside. Agnes was nowhere in sight, but I did spy the skinny woman I'd seen with her at the first protest. Hurrying over, I waited until the woman finished dishing out some mac and cheese to a student and then smiled at her.

"Hi," I said. "You don't know me, but I'm an acquaintance of Agnes Fitzgerald's. Do you know if she's working today?"

"Agnes? No, she's off today—be in tomorrow lunch, though," the woman replied, dropping her spoon back into the vat of noodles.

"Oh, that's too bad. I really do need to speak with her—you don't happen to have her home phone number, do you?" I asked.

The woman shrugged. "Nope. Agnes doesn't socialize much with anyone at work. Likes to keep to herself. You could probably ask at the main office, though. They might have it."

I thanked her and moved on, deciding there was an easier way to get Agnes's number. As I stepped away from the line to a quiet spot behind some trash bins, I punched in Shannon's home number.

"Yo, party central," a voice answered after half a ring.

"Shannon?" I said in surprise. "Wait, aren't you supposed to be grounded from the phone?"

"Nancy? Is that you? What do you want this time?" Shannon instantly sounded defensive. "And for your information, I picked up by accident. You know—like, force of habit or whatever."

Yeah, right. "Is your mother there?" I asked.

"No. Why? What do you want to talk to her about?" Now she sounded downright hostile.

"I just need your Aunt Agnes's phone number, that's all," I replied soothingly. Suddenly remembering that Mrs. Fitzgerald had mentioned that Shannon and Agnes were close, I added, "Do you happen to know it?"

"Of course. I can give it to you—but only if

you promise not to tell my parents I answered the phone."

I rolled my eyes. "Fine, I promise." For a second I wondered uneasily if Shannon was doing anything else that went against her grounding, like using the computer. . . .

But I shook off the thought quickly. Shannon definitely wasn't UrNewReality, and neither were any of her friends. For one thing, none of them were old enough to drive, unlike whoever had hurled that rock at me last Sunday evening.

Shannon gave me the phone number. "But she probably won't talk to you," she warned. "Aunt Agnes hates everyone. Well, except for me, of course." Her voice turned smug. "She thinks I'm pretty much perfect. In fact, she was the one who helped me make my BetterLife avatar as totally awesome as I am in real life. Not that it does me much good now . . ."

"Thanks, Shannon," I said, ignoring the not-so-subtle gripe. "Good-bye."

I hung up and glanced across the dining hall. Bess and George had already found the Nickersons and the al-Fulanis. All of them were standing around chatting near the entrance to the cafeteria line. I figured that gave me time for one more call. . . .

As predicted, Aunt Agnes sounded less than thrilled to hear from me, though she did seem to remember who I was. When she heard my question, she was silent for a moment.

"Oh, yeah," she said at last. "Come to think of it, I did see someone that day. Caught him looking out at me from behind a tree across the street while I was driving off."

My breath caught in my throat. "Do you remember what he looked like?"

"Yeah, I guess. Kind of a skinny teenage kid, dark skin and hair. Couldn't really see much else."

"Thanks," I said. "That's very helpful. Let me give you my number, okay? Please call me if you remember anything else." I recited my cell phone number twice, though based on her answering grunt I wasn't fully convinced she'd bothered to write it down.

I hung up and glanced across the room. Ibrahim was talking to Bess at the moment, laughing at something she'd just said. A skinny kid with dark skin and hair . . .

But I shook my head, instantly dismissing the thought. Ibrahim couldn't be the person Agnes had seen. Ned had been picking him up at the coffee shop at the time. Besides, I still couldn't

138

believe he'd vandalize my car or do any of that other stuff.

Plus whoever called the pizza place was female, I reminded myself. *I wonder if the figure Agnes saw could have been a girl?*

I almost called her back to ask. But Mr. Nickerson spotted me at that moment and waved me over. Putting away my phone, I hurried over to join the party.

After lunch, while Ned and his parents were still chatting with the al-Fulanis, my friends and I excused ourselves and hurried off to the library in search of a computer terminal. Bess and George were eager to check on our new creation, but I was already wondering if we'd been foolish to hide our identity this time. After all, most of our clues so far had come from UrNewReality's e-mails. How were we supposed to proceed if he/she/it couldn't find us anymore?

Not much had changed since last we'd seen Virtual River Heights. We'd left Dancin4Evah at the smoothie shop, and he was still there slurping down a wildberry smoothie.

"Now what?" George said as she activated him.

I bit my lip, feeling frustrated. "This investigation is going nowhere fast," I said. "We need help—and I know where we might be able to find some. Run a search and see if ParteeGrl21 is online. She claimed to be an expert on BetterLife, remember? Maybe she'll have some new ideas."

George seemed slightly insulted that I was going to someone else for computer-related help, but she searched and discovered ParteeGrl21 at the mall food court. We took Dancin4Evah there and approached her.

HI! Dancin4Evah said. CAN I TALK TO YOU?

SORRY, ParteeGrl21 typed back. UR NOT MY TYPE.

The miniskirted avatar started to walk away. I grimaced, realizing she had no idea this pierced-and-stylin' guy was me. WAIT! Dancin4Evah said, switching from public speech mode to private message. IT'S ME—VIRTUALNANCY. I MADE A NEW AVATAR.

ParteeGrl21 turned to face me. NANCY, IS THAT REALLY U?

IT'S ME, I said. MY OTHER SELF WAS TERMINATED. I NEED YOUR HELP TO FIGURE OUT WHO DID IT.

I know, I know—that was a touch melodramatic, considering we were talking about virtual people. But I figured it might catch ParteeGrl21's attention, and I was right. Her speech was peppered with multiple OMGs as she immediately offered to help in any way she could.

"Now what?" Bess asked, watching over my shoulder. "You're not going to tell her the truth, are you? You don't even know who she really is."

"I know. Don't worry, I've got a plan—just watch."

I typed fast, explaining to ParteeGrl21 via private message that I still suspected someone was impersonating my real-life boyfriend on the game. I NEED TO FIGURE OUT WHO IT REALLY IS, I went on, TO FIND THE REAL PERSON BEHIND THE AVATAR.

WHAT DO U WANT ME 2 DO? she asked.

FIND NEDNICK02, I replied. SEE IF YOU CAN GET HIM TO TELL YOU WHO HE IS.

She agreed and set off. It wasn't easy to keep Dancin4Evah unobtrusive, but I did my best, guiding him along at a safe distance behind her.

NedNick02 was at the public basketball courts watching a game. ParteeGrl21 walked over to join him.

HI, she greeted him. REMEMBER ME? WE MET @ THE PROTEST LAST WKEND.

HOW COULD I 4GET? NedNick02 responded right away. UR HOTT!

THX. U2, ParteeGrl21 replied. I THOUGHT MAYBE WE COULD HANG OUT SOMETIME.

KOOL, NedNick02 said. HOW ABOUT NOW?

ParteeGrl21 giggled.

"Hey, I didn't even know avatars could do that," Bess commented. "We could have used that giggle function when we were trying to get into that party."

"I knew about it," George said. "I just figured VirtualNancy wasn't the giggling type."

OK, THEN TELL ME ABOUT YRSELF, ParteeGrl21 was saying to NedNick02. I HEARD UR A COLLEGE BOY. I LIKE SMRT BOYZ.

"Good line," Bess commented.

I gasped. "It's her!" I blurted out.

"Huh?" George said. "It's who?"

I stabbed a finger at the screen. "I never told ParteeGrl that Ned was in college. I'm sure of it! In fact, she doesn't even know how old *I* am—in real life, I mean."

Bess looked confused. "So?"

"So don't you get it?" I cried. "She knows Ned's a college student even though I never told her. ParteeGrl21 must be UrNewReality!"

VIRTUALLY BUSTED

"**W**hat? Are you sure?" Bess sounded dubious. "I mean, the NedNick avatar looks sort of college-age-ish. Maybe that's why she said it."

"Anyway, just because she knows that it doesn't mean she's UNR," George added. "Maybe she saw it on NedNick's profile."

"It's not on there—I checked it out once and it's totally blank." All my instincts were pinging, and I was sure that I was right about this. "And the old VirtualNancy was a middle schooler, remember? So why would ParteeGrl assume my real-life boyfriend was in college?"

"Okay, whatever. So ParteeGrl21 is UrNew-Reality." George shrugged. "What good does that do us? We still don't know who she really is."

Bess nodded, glancing around the library at some of the students studying nearby. "Are you planning to track down every pre-med college girl in the greater River Heights area and demand to know if any of them are UrNewReality?"

"I don't think that will be necessary," I said thoughtfully, staring at ParteeGrl21. She was still trading lines with NedNick02—mostly just silly, flirty stuff. "I have an idea. Bess, can I borrow your cell for a sec?"

"Why? You didn't manage to break yours again, did you?" George asked as Bess handed over her phone.

"No. I just don't want my name showing up on caller ID." I flipped open my own cell phone and checked for the right number, quickly tapping it in on Bess's keypad. "As soon as I start talking, have our avatar interrupt and start talking to ParteeGrl, okay? Let me know if she answers."

"Okay," Bess said, looking confused.

I got up so they could take my place in front of the keyboard. Now that I was pretty sure I'd figured out ParteeGrl21's real-life identity, I didn't want to wait to confirm it. I'd explain everything to my friends once I knew for sure.

I dialed the phone and waited. "Uh, hello?" a gruff voice answered after a few rings. "Who's this?"

"Hello, Ms. Fitzgerald," I said. "Sorry to bother you again. This is Nancy Drew—we spoke a couple of hours ago, remember?"

"Oh." Agnes sounded decidedly underwhelmed to hear from me again. "Uh, I'm kind of busy right now. . . ."

"This will only take a moment," I said in my most ingratiating voice. "See, I'm very interested in that boy you said you spotted outside Shannon's house, and I wanted to ask you a few more questions."

"I already told you," she said. "I didn't get a good look at him."

I shot a glance at George, who was bent over the keyboard typing away. "I understand that," I said to Agnes. "But I'm working on a theory, and I just wanted to know if there's any way you think he might have been, you know, non-American?"

"Oh!" Suddenly she sounded much more interested. "Now that you mention it, it's definitely possible. Probable, actually. He had that look about him."

"I see." I glanced at George again, searching my mind for another question that might keep Agnes talking a little longer.

I needn't have bothered. "And you know, the way things are going lately, it's getting easier and easier to spot 'em," Agnes went on. "I mean, every time you turn around there are more foreigners in River Heights, taking our jobs and stirring things up. I tell you, it's enough to make you wonder if there's anyone left in their own country. . . ."

I let her rant on, covering the phone with my hand. "What's happening?" I hissed at George.

"Nothing," she whispered back. "Neither ParteeGirl or NedNick are responding to anything I try to say to them."

Bingo, I thought.

Lifting the phone again, I interrupted the ongoing rant. "Excuse me," I said. "I have another call. I'd better go."

I hung up the phone and smiled. Bess and George were staring at me.

"Aunt Agnes?" Bess said. "But how did you know?"

"There were a lot of little clues, and they finally came together for me," I replied, handing back her phone. "Plus, I realized Agnes has a motive."

"Shannon?" George guessed.

I nodded. "She must be harassing me because I busted her 'perfect' niece. And it probably didn't help that I was spending so much time with Ibrahim and his family, either."

"What do you mean?" George asked.

I gestured toward the computer. "Do me a favor. Run a search for Agnes's name on the *Bugle*'s website."

George did as I requested. It was only a matter of seconds before she'd pulled up a whole page of Agnes's letters to the editor, dating back several years. Most of them were complaints about foreigners, immigration, and similar topics.

"So she's one of the town cranks." Bess scanned the letters and shook her head. "But then why did she jump in to save Arij that time?"

I'd already thought about that. "I'm not sure she did," I said. "Nobody else saw that alleged red laser dot, right? She might have just seen a chance to avoid my questions and cause some trouble for the al-Fulanis at the same time."

"Whoa." George whistled. "So she's not just a crank. She's a total bigot and major troublemaker! Arij could've been hurt."

"So could Nancy," Bess reminded her. "Agnes must've thrown that rock at the overlook, too."

"I know." I bit my lip and stared at the computer screen. "The trouble is, I'm not sure how we're going to prove anything."

"But we have to," Bess said. "We can't let her get away with this!"

George smiled. "Hang on, don't panic. I have an idea. . . ."

"Good thing the big subscription launch doesn't happen for a few weeks and the game is still free," George commented a little while later. "I'd hate to have to pay for all these new avatars."

"You hate to have to pay for anything," Bess pointed out.

George stuck out her tongue at her cousin. I ignored them, leaning forward for a better look at the new avatar we'd just finished creating. This one was a young male character with dark hair and eyes and olive skin.

"Looks just like Ibrahim," I said.

"It's like looking into a mirror," Ibrahim agreed.

I glanced over at him and smiled. After hearing George's plan, I'd run over to the dining hall to see if Ibrahim was still there. Luckily he was, and once I'd explained the whole situation he'd eagerly agreed to do anything he could to help.

George sent the avatar, who we'd dubbed TehranBoy, into Virtual River Heights. We'd put Dancin4Evah on inactive status some time earlier, telling ParteeGrl21 that I had to get offline because I was going out of town for the afternoon.

"May I do the typing?" Ibrahim asked as George ran a search and found that ParteeGrl21 was still on active status and was back at the virtual mall. "It will sound more convincing that way, no?"

"Sure, good idea," I said. "Just remember the plan."

Ibrahim took the seat George vacated in front of the keyboard. "I remember," he said.

Soon TehranBoy was approaching ParteeGrl21. HI! he said to her. I THINK I KNOW U.

I DON'T THINK SO, she replied.

"Switch over to private mode," I suggested, peering over Ibrahim's shoulder.

He nodded and did so, then started typing again. I held my breath, hoping we could pull this off. *Otherwise, we're in trouble,* I thought. *If we blow this, Agnes will know we're onto her, and then we might never be able to prove anything.*

I KNOW WHO U R IRL, TehranBoy said. PLZ DON'T BLOCK ME UNTIL I TELL U Y. OTHERWISE I'LL HAVE 2 POST IT IN PUBLIC.

WHO R U? ParteeGrl21 demanded. TELL ME, OR I'LL REPORT U!

"Careful," George murmured. "We have to reel her in before she bolts."

I THINK U KNOW, TehranBoy responded. IF UR NOT SURE, MAYBE U CAN ASK MY SISTER NEXT TIME U SHOVE HER DOWN THE STEPS.

I held my breath. Would Agnes take the bait, or would she block TehranBoy from talking to her and disappear?

There was a long pause, but finally more text appeared in ParteeGrl21's text box. WHAT DO U WANT? she asked. Y DON'T U GO BACK 2 IRAN & STOP BOTHERING PPL?

"Nice," George said with a grimace.

I KNOW WHAT U DID TO N DREW, TehranBoy said. & I HAVE PROOF, 2. BUT DON'T WORRY, I WON'T TELL ANY1 . . . IF U GIVE ME $100 IRL.

THAT'S BLACKMAIL! ParteeGrl21 shot back immediately.

I KNOW, Ibrahim typed back. ISN'T THE USA GR8?

Bess laughed. "Good one."

"Thank you." Ibrahim looked up and grinned. "I thought so!"

"Focus," I reminded them, still worried that Agnes would sign off and disappear. After all, we were bluffing—if she refused a real-life meeting, we still wouldn't have any actual proof.

This time there was a long, long pause. IT'S A DEAL, ParteeGrl21 responded at last. MEET ME AT THE CURVE IN THE RD BY THE OVERLOOK ON RIVER RD. I'LL B THERE AT 7 2NIGHT W/THE $$.

"Bingo," I said out loud, finally relaxing. "Now come on. We have a couple of hours—there's one more thing we have to do, and we don't want to be late for that meeting."

"See anything yet?" George stuck her head out from behind a large oak tree and peered down the road.

"Shh. Stay out of sight," I hissed at her from the next tree over. We were just around the steep curve from the picnic spot. It was about two minutes to seven, and the rapidly fading light made it difficult to see anything more than a few yards away. I could barely see the outline of a slender, dark-haired boy standing at the edge of the road facing in the direction of town.

Was this going to work? I'm not the superstitious type, but I couldn't help crossing my fingers just in case. If Agnes didn't show, or got suspicious before doing anything incriminating . . .

George had ducked out of sight again and I

couldn't see her. Looking the other direction, I could barely see the top of Bess's blond head behind a patch of bushes.

Just then came the roar of an engine in the distance, and I turned to look down the road again. Headlights appeared, moving very fast—too fast for the curvy road.

I held my breath, squinting to try to make out the outline of the vehicle. It looked big and boxy, just as I'd expected.

Here she comes, I thought. *Does she see Ibrahim standing there?*

I got my answer almost immediately. With another roar, the van accelerated even more, veering off the road and slamming right into the figure standing at the curve!

DOUBLE TROUBLE

The van skidded to a stop with a squeal of brakes, almost sideswiping a couple of trees in the process. "Come on!" I shouted to my friends, jumping out from my hiding place.

Bess, George, and Ibrahim did the same. That's right—Ibrahim. See, that wasn't him standing at the edge of the road. It was a life-size cardboard cutout we'd mocked up quickly in the university art department. We'd counted on the fact that the light would be bad enough to trick Agnes into thinking it was a real person—the same way she'd probably been counting on that same poor lighting to claim that ramming into Ibrahim was an accident in case she got caught.

When Agnes climbed out of her van and hurried back to look at what she'd just run over, she got a big surprise. Not only were my friends and I waiting for her, but so were several members of River Heights's finest. Even though Chief McGinnis had been extremely skeptical when I'd called him, he'd agreed to send a couple of men out with us just in case. Hey, what can I say—he's learning!

"No!" Agnes blurted out in surprise as the uniformed officers emerged. "What's going on? It was an accident, I swear!" Then she turned her head and spotted me. "You!" she spat out, practically snarling with rage. "Why, you little . . ." There was more after that, but nothing I'd care to repeat.

"That's enough, ma'am." The senior officer, a burly man named Franklin, reached for his handcuffs. "I think we'd better take a little trip downtown for questioning."

I stepped forward and peered into the passenger-side window of her van. "Don't forget to grab that laptop when you take her in, guys," I advised the officers. "I suspect there will be some evidence we need on there."

"Wow. I can't believe we're finally alone." Ned smiled and glanced around River Heights's nicest Italian restaurant. The two of us were in a cozy booth in the corner, the faint sounds of soft music and the clink of silverware serving as background to our conversation. "I keep expecting you to have to rush off to investigate something else."

"Me too. Sorry about that." I lifted my water glass and touched it to his. "But don't worry, this case is definitely over now."

He shook his head, his eyes twinkling. "And you did it again. Another bad guy is off the streets—and the Web—thanks to our own intrepid investigator, Nancy Drew."

I took a sip of water. "Yeah, the Web part still feels weird to me," I admitted. "I wasn't sure we had enough evidence against Agnes in the real, three-D world—after all, you can't exactly throw someone in jail for running over a piece of cardboard."

Ned smiled. "Good point. But what about all those online threats?"

"I wasn't sure we could get that stuff to stick," I said. "At least not without cooperation from the creators of BetterLife, and we already know they're probably not willing to invade their users' privacy for silly stuff like, you know, solving a criminal case."

We'd both attended a lecture by the creators of BetterLife back when I was investigating Shannon's bullying problems. The two men had practically had a heart attack when I'd suggested it might be a good idea to run background checks on their users to avoid situations like the one Shannon had found herself in.

"Good thing Agnes cracked under pressure, then," Ned commented.

"I know. She started confessing even before they got to the police station last night," I said. "She even voluntarily ratted out her friend LuAnn Carter for making that threatening call to Professor al-Fulani's office, hoping it would buy her some leniency on her own crimes." I shook my head, glad that that part of the case was closed, too, but still amazed that even one of our town cranks would do such a thing. "Anyway, Agnes admitted she started harassing me on BetterLife as soon as she heard about what had happened with Shannon, hacking my avatar and my e-mail account, faking that video, and using a bunch of her own avatars to spy on me—ParteeGrl21, NedNick02, and even KrazeeBiker."

"What about that Guitar Lover guy and UNR?" Ned asked.

I shook my head. "She wouldn't 'fess up to either of those." Indeed, Agnes had insisted she had no idea who Guitarlvr15 or UrNewReality were, but that she'd noticed Guitarlvr15 hanging around a lot.

"Well, maybe it was Rebecca sneaking around to get online despite her grounding, like Agnes said."

"Maybe." I picked up my fork and poked at my food, feeling vaguely troubled. Clearly Shannon had filled her aunt in on that detail as well—Agnes had all but admitted she'd been planning to make some trouble for the avatar she'd assumed was Rebecca once she was done with me.

"So what about Shannon?" Ned asked. "Do you think she was involved?"

"No, I'm pretty sure she had no idea what Agnes was up to." I thought back to when the police and I had gone to tell the Fitzgeralds that Agnes was in custody. "She seemed pretty shocked, actually. Kind of turned white and kept muttering 'I knew she was nuts, but this is *nuts*.'"

Ned chuckled. "Very eloquent."

"Yeah. Accurate, too. As you've probably already guessed, Agnes overheard you and Lyle talking about our picnic at the overlook that day in the cafeteria."

"I didn't even notice her listening," he admitted.

"Well, that's how she got away with this—she wasn't all that noticeable. I mean, who'd ever guess that someone like her would even know one end of a computer from the other, let alone be some amazing super-hacker? I think George was actually a little jealous when she realized." I set down my water glass. "Actually, that was one way I was so sure I was right even before we proved it. I remembered the first time I met Agnes, when Shannon's mom knew what my BetterLife avatar had been up to even though Shannon was banned from the computer and couldn't have told her. Agnes must have filled her in right before I got there."

Ned looked impressed. "Good catch."

"I only wish I'd caught on sooner." I sighed. "It also took me a while to realize that Shannon told me her aunt had helped her with her avatar. Another real-life clue that slipped past me for a while."

"Hey, cut yourself some slack. It's hard to solve a mystery in two worlds at once." Ned grinned and reached across the table, squeezing my hand in his. "Anyway, I'm just glad it's all over."

"Me too." I squeezed back, feeling a flutter of

happiness. The first thing Ned and I had done that evening was talk out everything that had come between us lately. As it turned out, he'd known all along that I had no romantic interest in Ibrahim. However, he still wasn't sure the opposite was true. At first he'd found Ibrahim's alleged crush on me amusing, but then he'd become concerned that Ibrahim might get hurt. That was why he'd advised me against spending so much time with him.

Obviously Ned had also known that the e-mail complaining about him was a fake. Still, I was actually kind of glad that Agnes had done that. It had reminded me not to take my wonderful, amazing boyfriend for granted. Mystery or no mystery, I was definitely going to remember to make time for him from now on.

I smiled blissfully across the table at him, wishing this evening never had to end. After all, we'd waited a long time for it. . . . I was trying to figure out exactly how long it had been since that picnic by the overlook when the ring of a cell phone interrupted.

"Is that yours?" I asked, reaching for my purse. A quick glance told me I must have forgotten my own phone at home.

Ned was already pulling his out of his jacket

pocket. "Hello?" Then he handed it across the table. "It's for you—George."

"Oh. Thanks." I took the phone, wondering why George would be calling at a time like this. She knew about this date, and how long it had been in coming. "What's up?" I asked her.

"Sorry for interrupting, Nance!" George exclaimed. "But this is important. You need to get to a computer—stat!"

"What? Why?"

"Just do it," George urged. "Check out BetterLife. Seriously."

She hung up before I could respond. I handed the phone back to Ned, feeling a flash of annoyance. "Well, *that* was mysterious," I commented. Then I told him what George had said.

"Guess we'd better find a computer and check it out," Ned said, already pushing back his chair. Did I mention he's a good sport?

The restaurant's owner was a friend of Ned's father, so when Ned asked if he had a computer we could borrow, we were immediately ushered into a private office behind the kitchen. I sat down at the desk and logged on to BetterLife.

There was a message waiting for me from a familiar name—Guitarlvr15. "Weird," I murmured, clicking to open it.

There was no subject line, and the text was short and sweet:

MYOB—OR ELSE.

"There's a link." Ned was leaning over my shoulder, and he bent closer to point to the screen. "There at the bottom."

I saw that he was right. Hoping it wasn't some kind of computer virus that would infect the restaurant owner's computer, I clicked on it. A new page loaded, this one packed with text in a small, tidy font—columns of text, pages of it.

"What is that?" Ned asked, sounding perplexed as we both scanned it. "Just looks like a bunch of mumbo jumbo."

I started to nod agreement, then suddenly gasped as I spotted a familiar name among the sea of words. "Not just mumbo jumbo," I said, staring at the name: CARSON DREW. "*Legal* mumbo jumbo. And there's my dad's name in the middle of it, see?"

My heart started beating double-time as I read more, not wanting to accept what I already knew it was. My father's legal files. All the confidential, super-important information relating to that big drug case he'd been working on for the past week.

Just then there was a beep. Clicking back

to BetterLife, I saw that a new message from Guitarlvr15 had just appeared in Dancin4Evah's in-box.

GET THE PICTURE? it read. ONE CLICK, AND THE WHOLE WORLD WILL GET IT, TOO.

"It's blackmail!" Ned said grimly as he read the message. "Someone's threatening to put these files online for all to see. Could it be Agnes again?"

But a quick phone call to the police station answered that question in the negative, confirming that Agnes was still safely in custody. She hadn't been near a computer since she was captured.

"So she really wasn't Guitarlvr15," I said, staring at the screen, with all my dad's sensitive information still blinking out at me. "She isn't behind this. And somehow, I can't imagine some tween girl like Rebecca doing it, either, even if she somehow managed to figure out I was Dancin-4Evah."

"So that means . . . ?" Ned turned to look at me.

I stared back at him. "It means the case continues," I replied. "And the stakes are higher than ever before!"

Help Nancy Solve the Case on Your Nintendo DS!

Family heirlooms are disappearing all over Twin Elms. The residents are counting on Nancy Drew® to solve the mystery before it's too late!

- ❊ Interview people and gather clues using the stylus to uncover the location of the hidden staircase.

- ❊ Explore the large and mysterious Twin Elms house and examine anything that is out of place.

Earn the top rank of Master Detective and find the stolen items!

Available Now!

EVERYONE

E
ESRB CONTENT RATING

Visit www.esrb.org for rating information.

www.esrb.org

Visit www.thq.com to learn more!